WHEN THINGS RETURN TO NORMAL

T. Lang Davis

WHEN THINGS RETURN TO NORMAL

T. Lang Davis

1/2/2019
Dear Bill & Sharon
Hope you enjoy my book on the porch in summer and by the fireplace in winter.
Your friend

The stories in this book contain fact and fiction. The facts
may include locations and events in history and in the life of the author.
Other than the author, all of the characters in this book are strictly fictional
and do not represent any individual live or dead.

Printed in Canada by Rapido Books

Paperback Edition 2018
ISBN 978-0-578-41217-7

Copyright © Theodore Lang Davis, 2018

Theodore Lang Davis asserts the moral right to be identified as the author of this
work. All rights reserved in all media. No part of this publication may be
reproduced, stored in a retrieval system, or transmitted, in any form, or by any
means, electronic, mechanical, photocopying, recording or otherwise, without the
prior written permission of the author and/or publisher.

*Dedicated to Mom and Dad
and my grandparents.*

The world stands out on either side
No wider than the heart is wide;
Above the world is stretched the sky,—
No higher than the soul is high.
The heart can push the sea and land
Farther away on either hand;
The soul can split the sky in two,
And let the face of God shine through.
But East and West will pinch the heart
That can not keep them pushed apart;
And he whose soul is flat—the sky
Will cave in on him by and by.

From 'Renascence' by Edna St. Vincent Millay

FOREWORD

This title was lifted from the dialog in the movie Beloved Infidel *based on the book by Sheila Graham, a controversial, 1940s-era nationally syndicated gossip columnist. It's a true-life story of her long on-and-off love affair with F. Scott Fitzgerald.*

In the movie, after a major argument and long separation with Fitzgerald, Graham begs Scott for a change of scenery, for a trip to Paris. But it was the middle of WWII, not a good time to travel, and Scott had a deadline for a new book. His response was: "We can travel, even go back to Paris, when things return to normal."

When I heard this, I was struck by his naïveté, being a worldly and well-published writer who, among other things, had written The Great Gatsby. *He was not considering that, especially after a world war, things can never return to the 'normal' we romanticize and think we can return to.*

It's said that writers often write to pass along their life messages and ideas. I hope mine are all clear, useful, informative, introspective, inspiring, and spiced with some socially redeeming value. Most of all, I hope they are entertaining.

T. Lang Davis

CONTENTS

I sneezed on the *Mona Lisa*	1
Musical miracle	7
A buck to boost the ego	13
A report from the womb	17
A-bout the man and the war	25
Mango beach bar	27
My name is Michelle	31
And you're the roasted chicken?	35
A shared and secret happiness	39
Becoming my comic book superhero	47
Croissant	53
Bus stop pathos	55
Break away	59
Hey, Jew!	61
Carlita's curves	65
Battery life	71
Bus pass	79
I loved the man	85
Flanken memories	89
Classic lizard	95
Buzz off	99
First and lasting impressions	103
Mourning Morning	117
Millions of trees will be saved	119

Fish tale	123
Buzz at the Red Lion Inn	125
Beyond the face	129
Beep, beep!	133
Passing torches	135
Time god	139
Passion hut	141
Suckers for the snow-covered beggar	143
If you see something, say something	155
Johnny be good	163
Morning glory	171
Talk of the town	177
The four-carat diamond pendant	183
The Pope's visit to Banja Luka	191
Froth of a nation	195
Huntington Station diner	203
The old boys' network	207
Little girls, past and present	211
Home in the Becket woods	217
Just watch me!	221
Tram people	225
Reality one, reality two	231
Swim tube	233
The heartless dialtone	235
The sailboat and the motorboat	241
The gift of closure	243
The Australian and the Rolls	257
Acknowledgements	261

I SNEEZED ON THE *MONA LISA*

I wasn't planning a visit to the Louvre, but the promise of a dry, warm refuge under the glass prism entrance enticed me out of the raw Paris rain and down the escalator to the main lobby of the legendary museum. I checked my coat and strolled through the most famous of corridors, the walls draped in dark, redundant, religious oils - some works by the great masters.

I thought that, since it was early, there would not be much of a wait to view the *Mona Lisa* again. Personally, I like to see and hear other people's comments about this postage-stamp-size priceless painting of such great fame. For me, it's akin to the emperor's new clothes syndrome, as everyone acts so impressed, manifesting great reverence for that pensive lady imprisoned under bullet-proof glass and plastic so thick it distorts her very essence.

To my disappointment, the line snaked back and forth across the grand hall. Bleary-eyed and nose running from a lingering cold, I felt reasonably strong and had not sneezed all morning, so I felt it acceptable to wait and observe the others in line. People waiting were from all over the planet and a dozen languages mingled and buzzed about as the line crept toward Mona. Sooner or later, I would be face-to-face with the Grand Lady. A gigantic mural of Ancient Rome covered the entire adjacent wall and I quickly became immersed in its thousands of fascinating details. After about thirty minutes, when my legs were growing numb and about to buckle, I found myself face-to-face with the legend.

Just as I was about to move on to let the next group view the most famous and priceless work of art in all recorded history, without warning, a purely involuntary and very wet sneeze escaped my nose and mouth. With unbelievable force, along with a great roar - to my and everyone's horror - an overabundance of wet particles spewed all over Mona and started to slowly drip down her face. Thank goodness the glass was bullet-proof!

As the wet stuff started to drip down, the guards stationed nearby, seeing and hearing the commotion, rushed in and grabbed me, shaking me by the arms, yelling and screaming something in French. The chaotic scene that the guards created for an involuntary sneeze was not pretty or deserved, but then again this was the *Mona Lisa*, the pride of France, painted by a famous Italian - the single most important draw to the Louvre. And, of course, this was the French playing out their dramatic role, so I understood the symbolic implication of me, a possible 'terrorist' committing this despicable act of phlegm.

I didn't resist or try to escape - that would make it appear as if the sneeze was premeditated. The guards were taking me outside to a waiting van and probably off to prison, I thought. I didn't have my coat and, while being manhandled, I managed to dig into my pocket for the coat check. I waved it in front of the kinder-looking of my captors. They changed direction and headed for the cloakroom, taking me straight to the head of the line, where I presented the official coat stub.

The cloak attendant, being naturally inquisitive, quietly asked the guard what happened and he blurted out something in French that included the words *Mona Lisa*. Everyone in earshot who understood French, including employees and visitors, gasped in disgust and disbelief, staring at me as if I'd committed a capital crime.

My coat arrived and the guards grabbed it to examine it, lest it contained a gun or any other evidence of my bad character and evil intent. They found the smoking gun. Having simultaneously reached into both pockets, they pulled out a dozen crumpled and wet tissues which, when they realized were full of my germs, they promptly dropped. Everyone stepped back as if they were live grenades. Clearly, I was sick and the wet tissues proved it once and for all.

They were not convinced or finished with me. They pulled me up the stairs and out of the Louvre. Dozens of inquisitive students and tourists watched as the police intervened and took over from the museum guards, roughly escorting me into the windy and still raw January morning. Two rows of police officers were posted along the route to the waiting van, dozens of blue and white lights pulsing for added drama. I was interrogated in French all the way to our destination, telling them over and over, "No French." It was cold in the van and the road was very bumpy; each time I would get ready to sneeze, the five officers guarding me scrambled for cover.

I was then standing in front of a droopy-eyed magistrate behind an impressive, erotically carved desk. He asked for my passport. I told him, "Hotel, hotel," and he turned to an officer and waved me away with the back of his hand, to get finger-printed and have my picture taken. I figured it was for Interpol or French Intelligence. I had a white band slapped around my wrist. I was prisoner A-43595468.

Then on to the interrogation room with Francois, an English-speaking gentleman dressed in very casual attire. I thought, "I've seen lots of crime movies, so I presume this casual dress is to make me feel at ease and spill the beans without them having to torture me."

Francois had a clipboard with lots of questions and methodically asked me the usual stuff, as well as my military history, political affiliation, religion, date, and place of birth, and all of the things that would be needed to determine if my sneeze was well-planned and vicious or merely accidental.

I explained to Francois about my cold and that it was an accident. He laughed, but I could not quite figure out if he was laughing at me, was convinced that I had an evil premeditated motive, or if he realized how foolish this whole drama was. Yes, I sneezed on the *Mona Lisa*'s bullet-proof and atmosphere-controlled glass cage! "Don't you people have more important things to do?" I thought.

They took me to a holding cell. I asked Francois what was happening as they locked me in.

He informed me that I would soon be transferred to the Bastille since involuntary sneezing on a French treasure like the *Mona Lisa* is a crime punishable by a mandatory one-year prison sentence, no trial required; and since there were many witnesses, it was clear that I had committed this involuntary crime. I was lucky because intentional sneezing is a two-year sentence. Curiously, they let me keep my watch but took everything else of value.

I curled up on the wooden bench, covered myself as best I could with my coat and cap to keep warm, and fell asleep hoping that this was just a dream and I would wake up in my hotel room.

MUSICAL MIRACLE

Helen's vibrating smartphone wakes her at seven-sharp on her fortieth birthday. She's been deaf from birth but hears in a fashion through tactile vibrations absorbed through her cheeks, thumbs, knees and, most often, through the nape of her neck.

Peter - Helen's best friend since childhood and, of late, her significant other - has planned an extraordinary weekend getaway for her birthday. They escape early from Manhattan on a crisp, cloud-free Saturday morning in July. They head north and quickly leave behind the oppressive city heat. They cruise silently on the picturesque smooth strip of asphalt known as the Taconic State Parkway, with only the sound and feel of the wind rushing in through the windows. Unknown to Helen, they are destined for the idyllic Berkshire Mountains in Western Massachusetts.

At noon, they arrive at their destination: the summer home and venue for the Boston Symphony Orchestra. Helen looks around, but still has no idea where she is. She taps Peter's arm, making a two-hand gesture and signing "Where are we?"

He shrugs and smiles whimsically, looking around as if he wasn't sure himself and feigns preoccupation with the parking attendants in their orange vests directing him to an open space.

Once parked, he pops open the trunk and - to Helen's surprise and delight - pulls out a picnic basket, cooler, large blanket, small folding wagon with burlap sides, and a large brown paper bag emblazoned with the logo for Zabar's, the well-known upper West Side Manhattan gourmet food store.

Taking in the sun's warmth and enjoying the view of the picturesque lake below, they walk slowly through the parking lot. Peter pulls the wagon over the grass and navigates it around the deeper ruts. They cross the road and arrive at the back entrance, where the friendly attendant scans their tickets, hands each a program and with a big smile says, "Welcome to Tanglewood. Enjoy the performance!"

As soon as Helen sees the picture of the orchestra in the program, she realizes where they are and breaks into an ear-to-ear smile. She turns to Peter, tears blurring her eyes as she reaches up to give him a big hug around his neck. She backs away and signs the familiar: "Thank you. I love you." He touches his heart as well with his right hand twice, smiles and points to her. They laugh and embrace once again.
Peter planned this surprise birthday weekend months ago and, as soon as the Tanglewood tickets went on sale, he purchased the best seats available in the music shed: fifth row center stage. As a bit of a ruse (he's known to be a practical joker), he doesn't head to the seats in the shed but puts down the blanket under a massive old willow tree instead, it's roots likely having taken hold during the Civil War. He has purposely positioned the blanket far from the stage for a spectacular panoramic view of the grounds and lake.

It's an hour before the performance and the massive lawn fills rapidly, covered with many hundreds of blankets, folding chairs, and people, people, people. Many classic red and white checkered tablecloths are positioned both on the ground and on low tables to keep the ants at bay. Each table and blanket is chock-full of picnic baskets, wine and plastic Ziploc bags filled with gourmet cheeses, cold cuts and an assortment of trendy, overpriced, organic crackers. Coolers keep the wine, soft drinks and water at just the right temperature for the hot and humid day ahead.

Helen may not hear, but her other senses are super keen and she's already become mesmerized by the sights and smells, and the comings and goings of the audience. She can see the stage from the blanket and secretly wishes they could be closer to the action, perhaps even in the music shed, where she could view the expressions and craft of the musicians, and hopefully experience a variety of personal 'musical vibrations'.

Peter sees Helen block the sun from her eyes with her hand, squinting and struggling to see the action on the stage, and he knows this would be the perfect moment to pull out the ticket so she can see that they *will* be in the shed. With a big smile and flourish, he presents the tickets to her. At first, she looks at him strangely thinking "it's not like him to try to impress me with the price of a ticket." She stares at the tickets for an awkward moment, looking for a clue and suddenly she gets it. SHED in bold letters on the tickets. They *will* be going into the music shed after all! "Wow!" she sighs and continues to sign: "How come we are on the lawn now?" pointing to the blanket and up at the tree.

He cannot sign very well, so he writes on the edge of the program: "Best of all worlds for you, my birthday girl! Let's enjoy some food, wine, and nature, and then we will go to our seats in the shed." Helen is aroused, exuberant and out of breath with excitement at Peter's thoughtfulness, and if they were alone, she would surely rip off his clothes.

The orchestra members continue to file in, finding their places, adjusting their seats and placing their scores on waiting music stands. Some are focused on last-minute instrument tuning and practicing difficult segues. Some are getting emotionally ready by sitting silent, eyes closed, as others review the music, their heads bobbing. Others chat with fellow musicians, each psyched for the event and acutely aware that, even though individually they perform an important role, it's the combined effort and excellence of the orchestra and maestro that produces a flawless, unforgettable performance and unique experience for the audience. After all, this is a top-of-the-mountain watershed venue with some of the finest musicians on the planet, and possibly will be a well-remembered moment in classical music history.

The cowbell rings over the loudspeakers for the last call. Everyone with seats in the shed walks briskly in before the attendants block each entrance. Thousands of men, women, and children mill around the great lawn and slowly navigate the edges of hundreds of blankets and folding chairs, returning to their own blanket hamlet of chairs, chips, cheese, wine, and beer.

The orchestra is now in place. Stillness and quiet replace chatter and movement, especially in the shed. The patrons up front are first to see the Maestro enter from stage right and all except the infirm stand to greet him with a long, exuberant applause. He bows in all directions and, as best he can, projects his sincere humility and appreciation for the honor of their accolades.

This is a crowd that has traveled from the million-dollar condos up the road and by car, train, and plane from around the globe to experience this event. The Maestro bows, again and again, each time in a different direction, then turns and sweeps the point of his baton from one side of the stage to the other, acknowledging the musicians. Yet more exuberant applause fills the air. The musicians bow and, as the applause fades, they take their positions and ready their instruments for the performance.

The Maestro again raises his baton slowly, gracefully, signaling to all the start of the first movement of Beethoven's 9th Symphony. It's a perfect rain-free summer day in Lenox, Massachusetts and there will be no distractions from the weather, only by infants occasionally crying in the distance, symbolizing new life on our planet - one of the best sounds the human race possesses.

Helen anticipates the conductor's every movement, 'hearing' the music in her body – the vibrations on the very high and low ends of the oscillating, scintillating sound spectrum. The singing violins, French horns, flutes, clarinets on the high end; the bravado of the kettle drum, bass trombones, and bass on the low end - converging and exciting both Helen's thoughts and libido.

It's now the second movement and Helen first focuses her attention on a young Asian woman with short blond hair sitting right off the stage in front of her, playing her violin. Helen is mesmerized by the woman's poise, her energy and her command of the bow as it dances over the strings, her fingers moving in a blur of speed and perfection.

A crescendo reaches a powerful pitch and, at that moment, the actual sound of music becomes clear to Helen for the very first time in her life. The music has traversed her non-functioning eardrums and reaches the audio cortex of her brain. The music lasts for just a few moments and disappears, leaving Helen craving more. She is returned to her world of silence and grasps Peter's hand for emotional support, hoping it will bring the music back again. But this does not happen. With the heightened senses that the deaf enjoy, she now becomes aware of the irregular beat of her own heart. The music softens to a slow, tender and dramatic passage, and

Peter now becomes overwhelmed by emotion, thinking, "I'd give anything if only if she could hear this beautiful music."

As all boats rise with the tide and toss with the waves, the audience is symbolically in a great ship in a sea of music that inspires and lifts all that can hear. But Helen is alone on her island of silence.

To the cheers and accolades of the audience, the soprano now makes her entrance, dressed in a dramatic skin-tight red dress, her golden hair swaying side to side in slow motion as she acknowledges and thanks the audience all around her. The glistening jewels decorating her floor-length dress mesmerize and disarm Helen who, without warning, faints.

The music continues and Peter, with the help of another patron, quickly carries Helen out to the first-aid tent adjacent to the stage. After some time, Helen regains consciousness, but not by virtue of smelling salts or oxygen; not by a shake or discomfort or pain; not by flashing lights or the light of the rising sun, or, for that matter, any of the things that bring a deaf person to consciousness.

Paralyzed with emotion, Helen's breathing almost stops as she holds her breath so as not to miss a sound. Her heart races, pounds. With her heightened senses, she *feels* the music as it pierces her deafness - emissaries of octaves reaching her through scintillating vibrations.

The theme of the *Chorale Finale* is dramatized by Schiller's highly emotional "Ode to Joy" - man's cry for hope during a time the planet was filled with untold human suffering, cruelty, plagues, long wars, religious unrest, and premature death.

Beyond any logical explanation, Helen can now hear the music in a normal fashion through her ears, even though she had no preconceived notion of what 'normal' would be. For

Helen, she has been 'born anew' and - this time – 'whole', with the gift of hearing most take for granted.

Now, Helen is awakened each morning by the sound of birds singing, by the shouts of children playing in the courtyard, by the beautiful patter of rain on her roof, and even the horn of an impatient motorist.

The vibrating alarm clock has long since been given to someone less fortunate as a whole new world has opened up for Helen. She has become adept at making and receiving phone calls, enjoying music, listening to the radio in the car and TV at home, and going to a movie without having to read the actors' lips. Her concentration has suffered, but that's a small price to pay for her new-found fifth sense.

Everyone wonders if it was something spiritual in "Ode to Joy" that was truly Helen's miracle, along with the spirit of Beethoven visiting Tanglewood from the grave to anoint Helen with the gift of hearing. He, if anyone, understood the agony of being unable to hear his own music – his life's work.

A BUCK TO BOOST THE EGO

Sheila could make instant hot chocolate at home, but if she did she wouldn't have a reason to stop at the General Store and show off her latest Marshalls outfit, $29.95 career high heels and sleek, chic - so she thought - *professional* hairdo.

Sheila had worked at the General Store for several years behind the counter serving coffee, breakfast, and lunch, as well as taking cash for beer and chips - all while making non-stop 'tiny-talk' with the locals she liked. It was clear to many that Sheila felt she was working below her station and that she had no patience for anyone that was outside her small circle of handpicked friends and regulars. She ignored and was indifferent to outsiders.

Through two pregnancies and the years before and after, she grudgingly - doggedly - showed up every day and ticked off the minutes and hours, smiling at those she liked and barely hiding her seething contempt for outsiders when they asked for service, a coffee refill or - "damn them pain in the asses" - extra butter for that intentionally thinly-buttered roll she put in front of anyone she didn't know or like. She didn't know me, so it was clear she didn't like me. After some time, I got it, and the feeling became mutual.

An office job offer came from one of her regulars. The guy had a business in town and this job allowed her to quit the General Store, earn a little more, and dress smartly. She thoroughly enjoyed making a grand entrance each workday morning at the General Store.

She thought that everyone she knew considered her move up to an office job 'a big deal', and she liked the attention and watched as her replacements recited the familiar daily platitudes. "Hi Jake, how are ya?" "Sandy, the baby's growin' soo fast - how many months is he now?" And the never-ending, "That'll be seventy-five for the coffee. Would you like anything else?" followed by a half-swallowed, "See ya' round. Have a nice day!" to those she liked.

Hot chocolate in hand, she exits the store and returns to reality. She slowly opens the creaky door of the rusted and badly dented jeep that she ended up with in the divorce settlement two years ago. She never knows if the car will start or if the grinding sound of the flywheel will be heard by those in the store. The engine grumbles and thankfully starts. Gingerly, she slips into first gear while quietly, under her breath, prays, "baby, don't fail me now," coaxing the hairpin clutch into first and moving her junk heap out of earshot so that the sound of her rotting muffler won't be heard in the store.

She reminds herself that, even though she no longer works at the General Store, she still has a long way to go to balance her checkbook and get out of the financial rut that her lame ex-husband - with his foolish purchases of expensive man-toys and junkets to Boston to see the Red Sox - has gotten her into. Even now, he's two weeks behind with the child support.

Monday through Friday, she pays her buck to morph for a blissful moment from who she still is inside, in the hope that one day she will be the person she wants to be and won't need to ever step foot into the greasy and depressing General Store again.

The hot chocolate is cold when she arrives at the employee parking lot. Every day she drops it, mostly untouched, into the trash as she enters the reception area. She proudly, confidently prances down the long hallway to an office she shares with six others, exchanging the usual morning greetings along the way, while dreaming of the day she will be liberated from financial stress; the day when she won't have to think twice about getting a new toy for her little boy or a visit to the nail salon; the day she will be able to take her kid to Disney.

It's the American Dream. The dream that keeps her going and going and going, day after day. Whether she knows it or not, it's her birthright as an American, and if she works hard, doesn't stumble or give up - is not indifferent to those around her - there's a good chance she will make it happen.

Understandably, she cannot be concerned with the millions around the world that struggle each day just to feed their family and have a safe place to sleep. She cannot be concerned with the vast migration of humanity that risks their lives to relocate to a place on earth with a future for them and their families.

That buck that she spends each day for a hot chocolate could feed a starving child somewhere in Africa or Asia for several days. She is luckier then she knows, not only because she will not starve or drown on a makeshift raft, fleeing from terror in the land of her birth. She has a wide horizon to look towards, a light at the end of the tunnel, a future. All she needs to do is stick with it and follow the light of hope.

A REPORT FROM THE WOMB

It's December 6th and I am what in the future will be known as a 'war baby'. In just a few months, I will be born. It's 1941 and World War II delivers a broad and indiscriminate dose of misery across the planet. There is little to celebrate this holiday season. Americans call on tradition to renew and strengthen family ties. They break bread, engage in holiday celebrations, exchange gifts, and put the dismal state of world affairs on hold until - hopefully, one day - *things return to normal.*

Everyone tries their best to be positive and keep the spirit of the holiday season alive. They bring their children and grandchildren to department stores to visit Santa, to peruse the endless aisles of toys and clothing, all whispering loudly, "Buy me, gift wrap me, place me with love under the Christmas tree or mail me to a loved one far away." Shop windows come alive with animated Santa's elves, reindeer, and electric trains for the kids. For the adults, there's the latest fashion, all sprinkled with sparkling fake snow, dancing among a million flashing colored lights.

They buy gifts they can't afford. They plan holiday family dinners, church gatherings and office parties. Painfully, friends and fellow workers are missing, some already known to be dead - others, their fate unknown. Everyone looks for ways to escape the daily hand-wringing caused by the newspaper headlines, radio reports, and non-stop war chatter in the streets, coffee shops, beauty parlors, trolley cars, around work water coolers, and in neighborhood pool halls and bars. It's endless and everywhere, so people escape to movie theaters hoping for a few hours of distraction, entertainment and, mostly, a break from reality. *The Maltese Falcon, Sergeant York, Dumbo* and *Dr. Jekyll & Mr. Hyde* are now on marquees in towns and cities across America. Ironically, after the coming attractions, the first thing a movie patron sees is the *Newsreel*, the predecessor to television news. It's 'a week in review', a drama-packed, grainy, black and white, and very loud news report.

Somber music in the background, the war correspondent narrates the wretched news and disturbing images without emotion. A captive audience, all but the very young are thrown back into the brutal everyday reality of people dying in Europe, how the Japanese are torturing their Pacific neighbors, how our brave young men and women (really, just kids) are suffering and dying far from home. Movie patrons are injected into the battles as the ear-shattering roars of bomb-laden planes blacken the sky, as hundreds of enemy and allied tanks move across the terrain from Europe to North Africa, all this now happening in the theater where all thought they could escape reality for a short respite. They are plunged visually into the despair and horror, and forced to witness cities burning, and freezing men, women and children without coats walking in a surreal stupor in search of food and temporary shelter from the brutal winter and bombs, just hoping to survive one more day.

Every day, thousands of soldiers and innocent civilians die from bombs, bullets, exposure, starvation and, of course, man's most despicable pastimes: torture and murder. War *is* hell as evil governments and their brainwashed executioners wake each day with a voracious appetite to kill, kill, kill for power, territory and their demented rationale of ethnic cleansing on a scale that makes the Crusades seem a minor battle.

"I Want You." The drawing of Uncle Sam, a wise, old man dressed from head to toe in the red, white and blue of the American flag, with his long, white beard pointing, presumably, at YOU and posted everywhere. If you don't volunteer on your own, as long as you are young, male and able bodied, the draft board - now desperate for more warm bodies to induct into the carnage - is on your heels. Young men of eighteen, really just boys, receive their 1-A status in the mail and are ordered to report to a local induction center for a physical orientation. If they pass muster, they are quickly placed on a troop train and on their way to three weeks of basic training on the hot, sandy tank trails of Augusta, Georgia or the buzzing mosquito marshes of Paris Island, Port Royal, South Carolina, to name a couple.

After totally inadequate training, the men graduate as 'three-week wonders'. America needs you to hold a gun for freedom's sake, to save the British, to save Europe from Hitler, from Stalin, from Mussolini and to ensure that American shores are not next. You may have an opportunity to return home before heading to war and you may get to kiss your family farewell in your stiff new uniform. You are scared to death and know that you may never return and see your family again

Daddy shakes with fear at every postcard and letter arriving from the draft board. Mommy, in her sixth month, is preoccupied with my kicking inside her and trying to avoid my grandma's non-stop doting. Her clothes are becoming tight and uncomfortable as I grow and she can only dream of replacing them with the latest fashions as soon as I'm born. She's not happy with what she sees in the mirror as her tiny waist disappears, even though she is happy I am growing inside of her. She flips the pages of the well-worn fashion magazines in the maternity doctor's waiting room and skims the latest hair styles, feathered hats and boas, admiring the current palette of nail polish and lipstick (brash and bright red). I am comfortable and content, and becoming more of a person each day. I can kick and wiggle my toes

Dawn, November 25th, 1941. Yoshi wakes, showers and puts on his uniform. Numb with fear, tears burning his eyes, he pushes aside the beaded curtain and enters the warm bedroom. With a kiss on her head, he wakes his wife Shiromi and together they softly shake peaceful slumber from their two little children. Yoshi alone knows that he will very likely never see his wife and children again. He tells them that they need to be strong and to take care of each other until he returns. They all begin to weep quietly into their pillows. He walks back through the beaded curtain into the tiny kitchen and holds the last family picture, taken just weeks ago on his daughter's second birthday. As he departs, he remembers that there are no copies. Softly, reluctantly, he places it on the kitchen table

On November 26th, 1941, Yoshi and the thousands of men comprising the Japanese First Air Fleet Aircraft Carrier Group depart Japanese waters armed to the teeth with thousands of bombs and torpedoes. Their ships cut through the icy Pacific waters and, in the name of Hirohito, their sacred Emperor Showa, they plan to fulfill their insane mission: Destroy America's Pacific fleet at Pearl Harbor. Bring America to its knees so it will not interfere in Japan's manifest destiny - the desire to expand its borders and conquer as much of the Pacific and the world as possible

"Aaron, come quick, we're under attack by the Japs!" my grandma yells to my grandfather as she is riveted to the radio. It is 2:30 on a quiet Sunday afternoon and my grandpa

rushes, confused and disoriented, into the living room, trips over the hall rug, and joins my grandma. Eyes popping, they gaze deep into the speaker of the large floor radio, as if it were a television screen of the future. They are shaken as they share this surreal and horrific moment in history.

Through the crackling static they listen to the voice of John Charles Daly, a well-respected war correspondent and journalist. You can hear the pain in his voice as his customary calm has vanished and he reports, "As I speak, the news is still coming in of an unprovoked sneak attack by the Japanese fleet on Pearl Harbor, our major naval station in Hawaii." He pauses for composure, clears his throat and goes on. "The early reports are that many of our ships have been sunk and others are still burning. Perhaps 2,000 or more of our soldiers and sailors have perished as they slept." He continues in an even more somber tone, "It's now clear that this brutal attack by the Japanese Empire will certainly force America to declare war and propel us into war in the Pacific.

On Saturday December 6th, 1941, Pearl Harbor was just another sleepy and mostly unknown military outpost in the Pacific. The following day, Pearl Harbor would never again be just some exotic way station in the Pacific, where America refueled and refitted its ships, and where G.I.s watched and danced the hula with Hawaiian girls in the local bars and dance halls. Pearl Harbor would no longer evoke thoughts of pearls or warm harbors in Hawaii. It would *forever* be a symbol to the American people of an unprovoked sneak attack and bring to mind those that died as they slept. It would be the ultimate warning that America must never, ever keep its guard down and never be complacent on account of its massive stores of weapons, ships and planes. During that period of isolation, America was not prepared to fight one war, no less two, and the Japanese knew this. There was much work to be done to prepare for the fight and it needed to be done very, very quickly. It was a matter of survival at this point in time since Japanese submarines had been reported off the coast of California. It is said that the Japanese could have probably gotten as far as Chicago if they had tried. Fortunately, they didn't or we may all be speaking Japanese now and answering to the Emperor of Japan.

Grandpa, an immigrant from Austria/Hungary, is now forty-four and I will be his first grandchild. Each day he rides the subway to his hand laundry in the basement of the Hamilton Hotel on the fashionable upper West Side of Manhattan. On the noisy, jerky subway ride from the Bronx, he reads the daily tabloid cover to cover.

It is early on Sunday morning, December 7th. Still unaware of the attack on Pearl Harbor, my daddy prepares to go out for the paper, a loaf of bread, and a quart of milk. Before he leaves, mommy places his hand over her round stomach. I kick his hand from within, he smiles with deep emotion and tears well up, but he says nothing, thinking, "The draft will get me sooner or later and, when it does, will I survive the war to see this child grow up? And what kind of world will it be? If Hitler wins, we're all doomed." He is not much of a communicator, so he bites his lip and leaves quickly rather than show much emotion to my mommy.

Later on Sunday, my mommy picks up the phone to call my grandma. Her neighbor is speaking on the party line and she hears the woman say, "The Japs bombed Pearl Harbor today." Without hesitating, my mommy breaks in, "Sorry to interrupt, but what's happening?" And since this is an unusual circumstance, the normal protocol of getting off the shared phone line is put aside, and the woman she knows only as Kate delivers details of the shocking news. Mommy forces out a thank you, asks Kate how long she will be on the phone because she wants to call her mother, and sighs, returning the heavy black receiver to the cradle. She wobbles into the kitchen to make coffee and lights a cigarette, pondering the future in this solitary moment. Little does she know that, one day, her cigarette habit will shorten her life and make her last years a paralyzed and living hell.

The phone rings. It's my Aunt Martha. "Stelle," she inquires in a low and controlled voice. "How are you feeling today, sis?" knowing that my mommy has been having a rough time both physically and emotionally. She determines that her sister is fine and then asks if she's heard the news yet. My mommy says, "You mean the Japs' attack on Hawaii?"

Fast forward 62 years…
I look into the open casket and see my mother for the last time. At 62, I wonder if - in a lifetime filled with good and bad, of great beauty and destructive vanity, of a youth filled with good health - she would be pleased to know how she looks this last time before the casket is closed and this chapter has ended. The lipstick is the same red - brash and bright - that she wore while she carried me; perhaps a coincidence, perhaps not.

Three months later, I watch the green line on the monitor become weak and level out and I've witnessed my father's heart beat for the last time. It's a surreal moment for a child and now I must accept that I've lost both parents within three months. For my sister, it's too painful. She holds her emotional pain in the waiting room. When I come to get her, she knows our father is gone and we tearfully embrace and now join the club of children with only memories.

America thought it rational to round up all Japanese Americans and place them in internment camps, and to then drop not one but *two* atomic bombs three days apart, incinerating millions of innocent human beings in the hopes of ending the war in the Pacific and saving the lives of our men and women in battle. What many Americans did not know was that one of the primary incentives to drop the bombs and end the war quickly was to prevent Russia from coming to Japan to help with the war effort. It was clear to Truman that Russia was not our friend and that they would complicate matters with a communist agenda, the way they were already doing in Europe. The bombs did end the war in the Pacific and did save American lives, but with a long-term price on humanity.

I often wonder if we could have ended the war by dropping just *one* bomb and waiting longer than three days to see if the Japanese understood more bombs would be dropped if they didn't surrender. I also wonder if President Truman had a child or family member living in the second city to be bombed, would he have waited longer than three days before dropping that second bomb or would he have targeted a different city? Perhaps dropping the bombs on Japan's most important military bases first would have convinced the Emperor to surrender, and millions of innocent lives would have been spared

I am now 76 and have lived a full, rich life. I think less about myself and more about the future of our planet, our children and their children. I turn on my radio each morning and hope never to hear of another Pearl Harbor or of another 9-11 - or even worse. I hope never to hear that a nuclear weapon, having fallen into misguided hands, has incinerated a city of innocent people ... in the name of someone's god or someone's greed or someone's inhumanity.

A-BOUT THE MAN AND THE WAR

My grandfather pulled the plug and carried the table radio from the kitchen into the den. He plugged it back in and settled into his La-Z-Boy recliner to listen to the second Clay/Liston bout in Lewiston, Maine on May 25, 1965.

After listening to the commentary and the initial few minutes of the first round, he noticed the signal had gotten weak and there was a lot of static, so he decided to move the radio back into the kitchen to continue listening to the fight.

He unplugged the radio and brought it back into the kitchen. It took him only a minute and, when he plugged it back in, a very excited announcer was screaming, "Ali is the Champ! Ali is the Champ!" You could hear the excitement of the crowd in the background. My grandfather, confused and disoriented, couldn't believe what he was hearing and turned the dials wildly, hoping to hear more about the fight. But after a few minutes, he had to accept the fact that the fight was over. Ali had won and he had missed a monumental, stellar moment in sports history.

It's now June 3rd, 2016. Today, newscasters around the globe frantically pore through their archives for those poignant sports history moments that represent the life of Mohammed Ali, considered by many the greatest athlete of all time. Each reporter was hoping to present the first, finest and most emotionally packed review of the man who bragged with good reason that he was 'the greatest'.

Ali was admired and loved by millions who had never met him or seen him in a live bout. He was also revered by those who shared and understood his moral rejection to fighting in the Vietnam War. Because of his religious beliefs, he was cruelly stripped of his titles and prevented from boxing - boxing being the only thing he was skilled at and the only way he could earn a living.

If you visit the Vietnam Veterans Memorial in Washington D.C., you will find - carved carefully in stone - the names of all the children, spouses and friends of Americans who, in hindsight, lost their lives in a run-a-muck war conceived and perpetuated by the egos of a few American presidents, their misguided advisors and hawkish Generals.

Several times over the years, I tried to approach the memorial wall, but each time emotion prevented me from getting close. I just couldn't do it. I finally got up the courage just two years before Ali died.

We have our families and our friends, we have our pets and our school memories, we have our milestones of birth, death, marriage, success, and failure, we have our vocations and avocations that are the mosaic of our lives and... we have our heroes. Yes, indeed, our heroes bring a special richness to our lives; they inspire us - we live vicariously through their successes, failures and human frailties - and they are at times our guiding light. They ground us, they make us feel good when we are down, and they keep us going when things get rough.

Mohammed Ali, you will be missed by all who knew you from near and far. I close my eyes and fantasize how it was back in 1942, when my mother and yours gave birth to us – just eleven days apart - and how they could not have conceived how different our lives' paths would be.

MANGO BEACH BAR

The red and yellow fireball slowly creeps out of the Mediterranean, promising another perfect summer day on the magical Greek island of Zakynthos. It's a summer paradise enjoyed primarily by Italian and Greek tourists.

A small hut with faded pink cement walls sits on the beach adjacent to a shabby bamboo bar. The Mango Beach Bar is a classic, circular bar with a weathered blue canvas canopy, sandy wooden floor and straw roof, additional shade provided by sun-bleached Pepsi and Heineken umbrellas. It's inviting any time of day or night for the casual drinker and diehard soccer fan.

Eight bar stools circa 1950, with pitted chrome and faded imitation patent leather seats, lean left and right in the sand. A satellite dish hangs awkwardly off the roof of the hut. The bartender's tools of the trade are strewn about, unwashed, just as he left them last night at closing, the liquor hastily locked in the little hut for the night.

A soft warm breeze rustles the weeds around an old adjacent RV, wheels half buried in the sand, and a rusted topless white jeep sits just feet away. The RV shifts slightly on creaky springs, as the sleeping bartender turns in the direction of the naked young woman - his last client before closing - who he charmed into sharing his bed.

His movements stir her and slowly she opens her eyes, looks around, struggling to orient herself to a place she's only seen boozed up in the dark.

Straw-thin rays of morning light enter through the corners of the stained brown curtains and, like spotlights, project onto the ordinary, making it all dramatic and artsy. The top of a beer can sparkles, soap in the sink glows, and hot pink panties are bathed in a solo spotlight on the floor. She stares at them for some time, trying to recall how she ended up in this bed with this stranger, but she cannot because she was obviously totally wasted - again.

For a moment she muses, "Just another experience to remember on this amazing vacation," and looks over and locks onto the sleeping face. She remembered him as being much younger - and better looking - last night in the subdued and flashing colored bar lights. She now sees his craggy, tanned and wrinkled face with white stubble and realizes that he's old enough to be her father. Not that it mattered much; it wouldn't have been the first older man.

What was apparently exciting last night, while removed from sobriety, was just chemistry inducing her to share a bed with a charismatic, silver-tongued bartender type. A total stranger.

Her feelings and thoughts take a left turn and now she's experiencing panic - combined with nausea and an aching groin. The thought of spending any more time under the wrinkled flesh of this drifter is *not* an option.

The RV shifts gently again on squeaky springs as a jogger passes and the recent Harvard grad, having come to her senses, nervously shoves her bra and panties into her bag, slips into her jeans and top, and quietly slides out of the camper into the blinding day, sand hot on her feet.

Mango Beach Bar… No mangos, just two bodies passing in the night. When the bartender wakes, he'll look for female flesh and possibly an encore, but will realize that she's gone – and last night's catch will fade, like so many, into the mosaic of a lifetime of one-night stands.

She quickly distances herself from the RV, never looking back, consciously considering Lot's fate lest she turns into salt. She will always remember his sleeping face, the heat building in the RV, the smell of last night's sex, and it's very likely that she will not share the details of her 'young woman's adventure' with anyone.

Years later, when she has a flashback while helping her daughter dress for her prom, she will smile and remain motionless for a moment, then quickly move on with her life as a doting parent, wife and musical director of a major American orchestra.

MY NAME IS MICHELLE

Kids of all ages climb onto the squeaky swiveling stools, twisting and twirling around endlessly, anticipating their ice cream sundae, milk shake, sugar cone or thick malted with a few pretzel rods to dip into the glass and savor - salty and sweet.

When the kids are at school, the stools are occupied by retired local tradesmen with time to kill - to read the newspaper and share local gossip and nostalgia with their pals, signaling the waitress from time to time to 'top off' their coffee mug.

Since 1947, this restaurant has been a welcoming oasis where parents treat their kids (and themselves) to a fun and filling meal that fits into their blue-collar budget. Everyone thoroughly enjoys the huge sodas, precooked burgers piled high with condiments, fried clams resting on a mountain of fries, anticipating their ice cream concoction of choice as the final chapter.

At one table, an emaciated, wrinkled-faced, middle-aged peroxide blond - with milky transparent and freckled white skin, a fading skull tattoo on her arm, sunken lips and jowls, no teeth - quietly spoons her clam chowder, masticating the potato cubes with her gums. Her seriously overweight male companion is tightly wedged between the table and the booth's back. He leans past his huge stomach, shoveling large quantities of onion rings and a giant burger through his greasy lips, intermittingly belching and slurping down the thirty-six-ounces of diet soda, his over-taxed esophagus forcing him to periodically stop the eating frenzy and allow the food and drink to find its way into his stomach.

A high-school senior working part-time and sporting a soiled apron and grease-stained pink sneakers arrives at another table. In her soft and friendly voice, she recites, "Good afternoon, my name is Michelle and I will be your waitress today. Can I start you off with a drink? Our soups today are clam chowder and chicken noodle."

At another table within earshot I hear, "Good afternoon, my name is Heidi and I will be your server today. May I start you off with some drinks?" Heidi is a nineteen-year-old high school dropout, a single mom with a one-year-old daughter at home, cared for by her mother while she works. There is no father in the mix; he joined the Marines six months ago and she hasn't heard from him since. There is no money coming from the father, so Heidi struggles to make ends meet, depending largely on her tips. Her dream is that one day she will get her high school GED, trade her apron for a nice skirt, and get a good job in an office where she can earn far more and not arrive home totally exhausted.

Heidi continues, "If you order the shrimp basket, it comes with our golden fries, two sauces and you get an ice cream sundae for just one dollar." The patrons – half-listening - are simultaneously flipping the pages of their menus, mesmerized by the mouth-watering selections teasing them from the greasy laminated pages. By the time the food arrives, they are famished and the first person starts digging in, even before the waitress has put the second plate down.

This is America doing America: the land of freedom and the opportunity to eat outrageously large portions of food that will make you fat, give you heart disease and diabetes, and be responsible for the ever-increasing number on the scale, the waistband, and visits to the emergency room.

Success for some is simply finishing high school and getting a steady local job. For others, it's a master's degree at an Ivy League college. For that high school graduate, it's a car – any car that runs - a little extra cash to go out Saturday night, and a cool new pair of jeans. Making ends meet, balancing the checkbook and living from paycheck to paycheck is the likely scenario for many years to come. For the aspiring college student, their expectations are nothing less than a spiffy late-model BMW, a nice house or apartment in a good neighborhood, a membership to the local golf or tennis club, money in the bank, traveling and dressing to the nines.

Even if your parents did not aspire to 'great things' for themselves and don't expect more from their children other than following in their footsteps and working at the local mill or diner, they've got a choice. Anyone can settle for this, but if you've got some smarts, you can break the glass ceiling and make life bigger, richer and far more interesting. My parents were middle class and expected big things from me.

America is a place where, if you really want to succeed and you have native intelligence, common sense or a reasonable IQ, you have a better-than-average chance to do so.

"How was your burger, sir? Can I get you anything else? Are you ready for your one-dollar sundae or would you prefer something different from our ice cream dessert menu?" She drops the massive laminated dessert menu and moves to the next table.

"Good afternoon, my name is Michelle and I will be your waitress today."

AND YOU'RE THE ROASTED CHICKEN?

The waitress double-checks her order pad. She looks at the frail, old lady in the blue polyester satin dress and inquires, "And you're the roasted chicken?"

Sadie looks up, forces a smile, raises her forefinger off the table and in an almost inaudible voice responds, "Please make it well done, but not dry."

"Yes, Ma'am," the soft-spoken waitress responds with a genuine smile, having a mother about the same age and understanding the challenges of eating at an advanced age.

Overlooking the beautiful, idyllic southern Florida Intracoastal Waterway at sunset, two wrinkled men in starched white pants and stained designer shirts butter their bread with the greatest of concentration. Jamie comments that the butter looks like cheap margarine. Long gone are the days when these titans of American industry and finance made brilliant, well-calculated decisions and amassed fortunes, changing forever the American corporate and financial landscape.

Sammy, staring out the window at the sunset asks, "Sadie, remember that restaurant we used to go to all the time? The fish place with the plastic palm trees on the tables and the free shrimp when we had to wait for a table? I just can't seem to remember the name of that place.

"Sadie, did you hear what I said?" Sammy continues, appearing to lose his patience. Sadie was now deeply involved with her salad, looking for the single cherry tomato she thought she saw when the plate was placed in front of her. Suffering from poor memory, Sadie forgot that it was already consumed a few minutes ago.

Sam was waiting for a response as he shoved a thick piece of soft Italian bread into his mouth, using his whole face to accept and devour it without a sign of enjoyment or satisfaction, already reaching for the last piece in the basket. Distracted by another conversation, he quickly forgets all about his question about the name of the fish restaurant with the free shrimp.

The sweet and compassionate middle-aged waitress arrives at the table and sets the large tray down on a tray stand. She picks up two plates and, with a big smile, approaches the table. In a soft kind of intimate gesture, she inquires, "Meatloaf?" Sam nods, reaching for his fork before the plate hits the table. "And you're the roasted chicken?" the waitress enquires again of Sadie who, never removing her hand from the table, looks up and wiggles her forefinger again. The plate is slipped quickly in front of her.

Sadie was a judge for forty-three years in the 5th district of Kings County, New York. She is now eighty-five and her skin is transparent, her eyes watery, and her scalp can be seen shining through her thinning, bluish hair. Bright red lipstick is smudged on her teeth and doesn't quite make it into the corners of her mouth. She stares intensely at her plate for a full minute with her hands at her side, making no attempt to reach for her fork to engage the food. There's dissatisfaction and disappointment written all over her face, but since this is normal, the others pay no attention as conversation stops and silent eating begins - with the exception of the chattering dentures and slurp of soup.

On the way home in the big, old Lincoln, Sam at the wheel, Sadie remembers Sam's long-forgotten question about the restaurant with the shrimp. She blurts out as if she had just been asked, "It was the Dogbay Restaurant."

Sam, concentrating on his driving, speeding along at thirty miles an hour in a fifty-mile-an-hour zone - and having long ago forgotten his question to Sadie - responds, "The doggie bag is in the back seat" as they drive slowly toward mutual senility.

A SHARED AND SECRET HAPPINESS

"Sixty. I am sixty today," mulls Chima, staring into the mirror, noticing the sharp wrinkles around her eyes and the fatty tissue hanging from her jowls. With her forefingers and thumbs, she pulls back her skin at the temple and jaw to see how she looked just a few years ago.

Feeling a bit old and melancholy and trying to cheer herself up, Chima thinks of the landmark moments of her life. The most recent: her son's marriage to a woman she wholeheartedly approves of. She reaches back further to the times she first held each of her children, having just pushed each into the world, and back still further to her courtship with Yomi and their beautiful wedding, when both her parents were still alive. Behind those thoughts there is a pang of guilt that often rests on her conscience, as another level of her consciousness says, "He was always second best in my mind, but, well, it's my life and they're my thoughts, and he is a good husband and wonderful father to our children."

Chima recalls how her mother lovingly wrapped her own delicate pink and white kimono around her trembling body - the same one that her mother had worn at her wedding. Chima muses how, one day, she might have the opportunity to take that same kimono and wrap it around her daughter's body. Still looking in the mirror, she lets out another deep sigh, experiencing flashbacks of other milestones in her life. At that moment, she misses her mother and father very much, and wishes that they could be here today to celebrate her fiftieth birthday. She looks out her window and up into the clear blue sky, sure that they are looking down seeing her now and she says quietly, "Hi Mom. Hi Dad."

She goes further back in time to when a Western man filled her life, first with great joy and then great sadness. Joy, when every moment together and every touch was beautiful beyond words, always emotionally packed with what had morphed from casual friendship into intense, symbiotic love.

There was an unspoken barrier in Japanese culture that prevented her from having the same intimacy with her husband that she enjoyed with the Westerner in her youth. It was accepted by most Japanese women that the man was the master at home and at work. She was also restrained by her culture never to show deep affection in public or private, never ever saying the words "I love you." It never went much further than "I want you to bear my children," "I enjoy my life with you" or "You are a good wife and a good mother." But the passion that comes with the words "I love you" never came through Yomi's lips; never in the twenty-five years of their short courtship and long marriage.

She knew he loved her and that he was a victim of their culture, but she still wanted to hear those simple words, which for a Japanese man there really is no true translation.

She loved the way the Westerner held her hand and showed her affection in public, and she was out of her mind with joy when he whispered in her ear "I love you so much; you make me so happy," as they walked in the busy Tokyo streets or sat in the park. It was a big thing - a very big thing - for a Japanese woman to hear such words of affection. It excited her both emotionally and physically, and she could not wait to be alone and passionate with him again.

Her sadness came when he had to leave. She refused to face the hard fact that the relationship couldn't go on and had to come to an end. It was far too painful for her to be rational and totally comprehend why the cards were stacked against them. She knew culture was not an issue and she believed - or wanted to believe at that time – that, since she had lived in the West for several years, she could easily move West and make her life with this man that she had so quickly and completely come to love. She remembered her words to him in a moment of passion: "I love you – will you please give me a baby?"

For the Westerner, who already had grown children, it was very painful to hear; but he knew he had to be sensible, even if she could not be at that moment of passion and confusion. He loved her deeply and knew it would be a big mistake for Chima to have a child out of wedlock with him: a child who would have Western features and DNA. He worried that her brother, her friends, and strangers may reject the child. In school, the other children would see the difference and could - innocently - be cruel. For him, it would be painful, knowing that across the sea he had a child that was growing each day without a father, and because it would now be more difficult for Chima to find a husband, she would likely have to support herself and raise their child alone. "No," he said. "If many things were different, then I would say yes. But this is crazy, Chima!"

Chima moves slowly toward her secret hiding place. Her heart beats faster and faster. Gingerly she tugs at the bow holding the rice paper package together. Inside are a CD and a photo album the man had given her, memorializing their wonderfully carefree days together on that magical little island, and their travels to Kyoto, to Osaka, to Yokohama to watch the Sumo matches. There were memories of Tokyo and Room 3165 in Shinjuku, where for two weeks they played husband and wife – she going off to her job each morning as he worked from his computer and anxiously anticipated her return. The evenings could not come soon enough and each night as she entered the room, they would immediately fling themselves at each other, as if they had been apart for months.

Most nights, they went out on the town for dinner and sightseeing, and when they returned to their room, they made love again. They often woke in the middle of the night and made love still again and, in the morning, she cuddled up to him, purposely waking him, wanting still more of him before going to work. She remembers that he was always willing and wanting as well.

Hot tears fall onto the faded rice paper, temporarily blurring her vision. In this trancelike state, she doesn't care about anything except the contents of the precious package. Now, on her sixtieth birthday, she only wants to remember and relive those moments of joy with the man that filled her soul and whose soul she knew she filled as well. Reverberating in her head are his words: "I love you like I've never loved anyone ever before in my life."

She turns the pages of the little album, softly grazing her fingers over his face on each page. She can recall all the events associated with each photo as if they had just happened. She returns to a morning long ago on that little island. They woke before dawn and slipped from the warm covers. They dressed and quietly slid the shoji screen open as families in adjoining rooms - separated only by rice paper walls - soundly slept. They stepped gingerly into the still darkness toward the outdoor showers, the crushed rock underfoot sounding like thunder in the predawn silence.

Once in the common showers, they removed each other's bathing suits and soaped each other's bodies, tickling each other, giggling quietly, their slippery bodies hugging and kissing under the warm stream of water - oblivious to everything on earth except each other. They patted each other dry and were now ready for the dawn.

They selected two bicycles and walked them slowly through the morning glories in the courtyard, around the stone entrance that keeps out the evil spirits, and past the shisa dogs that were guarding the home from the corners of the red ceramic roof.

Breathing in the sweet smell of dawn, their souls entwined, they pedaled quietly, peacefully through the thick, grey morning mist. With each stroke of their pedals, a sense of absolute joy rose. Joy to be alive and joy at being together.

Within minutes of reaching the beach, a sliver of red appeared on the horizon, slicing the black sea from the black sky, defining morning. At that very moment, the sounds of songbirds filled the air, roosters crowed, and all living things shared the beauty and tranquility of this magical little island.

The moment was so incredibly, intensely clear, that each of them would be able to recall it at will, exactly the way it was, as long as they both would live. It was their window into a shared and secret happiness.

Before closing the album, she thought of the time they visited a suburb of Kyoto and stayed at a traditional Japanese inn, a ryokan. They slept on the floor on a comfortable mat placed over tatami flooring.

They woke very early. He pulled her out from under the covers and asked her to stand in front of a full-length mirror - and to keep her eyes closed. He removed her nightgown and draped something soft and silky on her naked body. It was a large silk scarf that he had bought for her from Liberty London, her favorite shop in the UK. It was printed with pastel pink flowers that matched her soft, pink skin. She opened her eyes and came close to tears. Joy was written all over her angelic face.

They put their robes back on and went together down the hall to a small room with a barrel filled with hot water. Robes once again removed, he latched the door, got in first and she slipped in, onto his lap, where they stayed naked and motionless for a long time, with only the sounds of their breathing, their hearts beating and the shrill mating call of the rooster down the road.

Chima now goes to the closet and removes the scarf from its original Liberty London box. She takes off her clothing and drapes the scarf on her body the way he had done so many years before. She stands in front of a full-length mirror for what seems an eternity, her arms wrapped around her body, weeping softly. Even though she is alone, she sees his reflection behind her, smiling his approval. She feels so safe and so whole and experiences an ethereal sense of peace. It was always this way - and she knew it always would be.

"One day I will hang a picture of you in my house and tell my children how you inspired me when I was a young woman," she recalls telling him. For this special birthday, she decides to treat herself to a very special gift, a very special version of their lives

"He did come back to me and he stayed - and these precious children are *our* children. While our children were growing up, we returned to the same little island every summer. He still fills me each day with joy and happiness, and I strive to fill him each day with joy and happiness. He shows me his love every day in so many ways and makes love with me with the same passion and sweetness as when we first met. I must still sometimes cover my mouth with my hand during lovemaking when our children are around, so they will not hear my unbridled passion. And we both feel so blessed and so lucky because we share and have always shared a beautiful life together."

East and West met, body and soul mingled… and their spirits and souls never parted.

BECOMING MY COMIC BOOK SUPERHERO

In a Korean documentary produced by the survivors of an ill-fated climb up Mt. Everest, the narrator speculated: "You only truly know yourself when you are in survival mode, when all of your mental faculties, physical strength and willpower merge as one." That is when the stuff of survival rises to the surface and that's the moment one discovers the truth of 'Who am I?' Will I save myself first or will I help another to survive at the risk of my own life? We likely won't know for sure until that moment of truth arrives.

It's the fall of 2002 and I've traveled halfway around the world on an adventure of a lifetime to trek up an 18,000-foot mountain in Nepal with an unknown guide and seven total strangers. For six months prior, life was all about planning, training, selecting equipment, getting shots, and reading up on the customs, terrain and weather of this mystical and little-understood region on the roof of our planet. Yes, I'd drafted and signed my will, had the required stress test and physical, and purchased MedEvac insurance.

For many months prior to leaving the comfort of my home, I lived in a constant state of anxiety, excitement and a looming ever-present fear of the unknown. Each day I questioned the sanity of my decision to commit to such a physically and emotionally demanding trip. Floating constantly in my head were thoughts of the bitter cold and the unpredictable snow storms that could last for days or a week, stranding us on an inaccessible mountaintop with the biting wind, lack of sufficient oxygen, and the possibility of mountain sickness. I was also concerned that the other seven unknown trekkers and our guide would be a good fit. I worried about the relentlessly steep periods of climbing and wondered if I would be able to keep up with their pace and not somehow get separated and lost.

Even though I was not climbing Mt. Everest, for me it might as well have been, because I drew comparisons to the well-documented, ill-fated tragedy described by the survivors of recent climbs and the popular book *Into Thin Air* by Jon Krakauer.

At 11,000 feet, the oxygen starts to thin, which is when some climbers start to feel the effects of mountain sickness. It gets harder to muster up energy and it's easy to get disoriented, so slips, falls and flawed decisions occur more frequently - and can have fatal consequences.

It took us almost a week of grueling physical challenges to get to Namche Bazaar, a village where even Mt. Everest climbers make an overnight stop before their death-defying attempts to summit the world's tallest mountain.

After leaving Namche Bazaar and trekking to 13,000 feet, we passed a monument to a group of Japanese climbers: a brass plaque engraved with the names of the men and women who had recently died in an avalanche on that very spot. It was a chilling reminder of the real dangers all around us, as we looked up and viewed the icy peaks hanging ominously above. When our guide suggested that we move along without further delay, we needed no convincing.

Some of the walking paths were just very narrow ridges and a slip or misstep on the loose gravel could mean falling hundreds of feet down a steep, sloping mountainside, possibly into the icy waters of the fast-flowing Dudh Kosi River. Chances are, no one would ever find the body.

Carefully, we navigated the primitive hanging bridges - some seemingly held together with luck - as they swung precariously in the wind. Most had weak, rotted or missing planks, and thin cables or ragged rope handrails. The handrails were positioned much too low for westerners, so we had to bend down while walking and this compromised our balance as we moved carefully - one terrifying step at a time - while the freezing river roared below us.

Our guide Chris was a British man in his thirties who, years before, had fallen in love with Nepal. Bitten hard by the beauty of the mountains, the wildlife and the rich culture of the people, he chose to break off his engagement and spend the remainder of his youth embracing and exploring the mountains, and learning the ancient customs of the Nepalese and Tibetan people.

Loquacious and funny, Chris was happy in Nepal doing what he loved best: taking groups of adventure seekers into the mountains and, between tours, living in Thamel, the colorful bohemian-style section of Kathmandu. In his free time, he put on his photo-journalist hat and worked on assignments for international travel guides and magazines. He was an excellent guide with a wonderful, cheerful disposition, and was laser-focused on our wellbeing: watching over each of us like a mother hen, checking how and where we climbed, and always looking for signs of fatigue and mountain sickness.

The day finally came when we would summit Gokyo Ri, which was 10,000 feet lower than Everest, but for us - untrained in and unequipped for serious mountain climbing - was *our* Everest. Of course, everyone was psyched, nervous, shaking and numb from the cold and lack of sleep the night before - but *ready as hell to summit!*

We started our ascent at first light and were instructed by Chris and the Sirdar (head Sherpa) to move slowly because, if we didn't, we would tire quickly and there was a far greater chance of fatigue and mountain sickness. From time to time, our group stopped to view the incredible, breathtaking mountains around us and the three brilliant blue-green lakes at different altitudes below us. We could see our camp, the tents, and yaks as they became smaller each time we looked back. The people below looked like ants and our tents were the size of raisins.

A Tibetan custom is to string colorful prayer flags made of strips of crude gauze-like fabric from one tree to another. They fluttered noisily in the strong wind and reminded us that they are intended to bring luck and to bless the countryside. We became one with the morning mist as it silently rose from below, followed us for a while, and then rushed past us into the sky.

Every climber will attest to this: reaching the summit was something that cannot be described but must be experienced. For a while, the sky was clear with intermittent cloud clusters. When the clouds dissipated, the sky opened and we gazed down at the frozen tundra and massive glacial moraine thousands of feet below us that had been gouged out by massive blocks of ice pushing inland. From our perch, we could see the blue-white clouds and weather system that often enveloped Mt. Everest, Lhotse, Makalu, Cho Oyu, and Ama Dablam - all mountains of incredible beauty and of equal or greater danger to climbers. Many skilled climbers and their well-seasoned Sherpa guides never returned.

Even though there were a few scary moments for me, it was during the daily climbs - when oxygen was thin, the weather was challenging, and the paths were slippery or gritty - that I was forced to look inward for mental strength and stamina. When my legs were fatigued and burning with pain and cramps, and when my lungs were gasping for oxygen and I wanted to give up, I involuntarily attained some mysterious form of inner strength that came, I think, from the essence of who I *think* I am. It's amazing how we can muster the adrenalin and strength needed to surpass our physical limitations. With survival - my only choice - I became my comic book superhero.

CROISSANT

Take the steep and narrow winding road up to the top of the mountain on the Eastern end of the Greek island of Zakynthos and you will find - perched on top - a surreal and beautiful hotel villa overlooking the turquoise Aegean. It was built by a wealthy Italian businessman who, at great effort and expense, transported all the stone and marble from quarries in Italy. The white and blue terrazzo tiles, produced by hand in Italy - each with a character of its own and representing the master's craft - were also delivered to the top of the mountain.

Fashioned after an Italian palazzo, this marvel was built over a six-year period, stone by stone, tile by tile, employing mostly Italian craftsmen brought in for the job. Since the Roman occupation of Greece, and because of its proximity to Italy, Zakynthos has retained much of its Italian flavor.

Each morning, from the panoramic windows of our room, the 'Eagles Nest', we would witness the breathtaking beauty of the sun, first peeking over the horizon from the sea below and then washing the white houses below with a golden hue. A promise of another perfect summer day.

I am hungry. My daughter is still sleeping. I pull on my swim trunks and slip quietly out of the room, moving with great anticipation toward the Greek/Italian breakfast buffet. Each morning, I look forward to a grand selection of delicacies, different from the day before.

Tempted today by a delectable presentation of calorie-laden croissants - some filled with nut chocolate and some with creamy custard - I must consider my expanding stomach. I know the logical choice is to select one, either nut chocolate or creamy custard, but definitely not both. It's almost impossible to pass these up and move on to the boring yet healthy cereal and fruit. Stoically, I select the custard croissant and, begrudgingly, some fresh fruit and yoghurt.

I consider my options and decide, "The croissant will wait until after I eat the boring fruit. It's my reward." The fruit is consumed rather quickly and now, for the *piece de resistance*, the top performer on my plate.

With a mouth-watering sound, the sharp serrated knife slices through the flaky, crunchy crust. I pick up the first piece and place it through my lips. The buttery crust is pierced by my front teeth and the sweet custard squirts into my mouth, super-energizing my taste buds. Truly, there are no words.

The experience is soon just a very pleasant memory and now the chocolate nut croissant calls out to me from across the room. Staying in an Italian villa, I recall the Roman poet Horace, who believed in enjoying the moment while you can and who said "Carpe Diem!" Seize the day!

No one will know. No one will care.

BUS STOP PATHOS

It's a cold Tuesday morning in January and I'm comfortable, warm and content at the Baker's Café here on Main Street.

The eggs would have been perfect if they hadn't arrived almost cold and - considering that this is a bakery - the bread was not stellar nor worth the carbs. I ask myself, "Why don't all restaurants have the sense to heat up cold plates so hot food is hot when presented? Two days in a row, the same scenario; first at Jake's Diner down the street and today at Baker's Café."

So how does one say to a waitress, without ruffling her feathers or getting a 'deer in headlights' stare, "Please have the cook heat up the plate, because I don't want my fucking eggs iced cold! And, while you are at it, this does *not* mean I want my cold salad on a hot plate just out of the dishwasher!"

Looking out the large window of the café and across the street, I see ten people waiting for the local bus, standing in front of the defunct family drug store that was put out of business some years ago by a 4,000-store drug chain. They are framed by three-foot-high piles of snow from yesterday's storm. A man in a thick red and black plaid lumberman's flannel jacket is sucking on a cigarette through his gloves. A short, hunched-over, old woman - a well-known local I'd call (tongue-cheek) a 'conduit for social intercourse and information' – animatedly makes small talk with the man to her left and the woman to her right, each politely listening with no real interest. Everyone in earshot is forced to listen to her loud, shrill voice; actually, it's probably helping take their minds off the cold and the lateness of the bus. Most appear frozen, uncomfortable, agitated and fidgety as they strain their necks every few seconds to see if the bus is yet in view. It's not.

As a wannabe photographer, I see a photo opportunity and bolt out to my car for my camera. I return to my cozy table at the window and compose a picture of the bus people in the distance, my coffee cup, empty plate, frilly tablecloth, and the plastic flowers on my table in the foreground, and the well-decorated Christmas tree just outside the shop window. It evokes such pathos; likely, all the people waiting are unable to afford a car or take a local taxi. My pictures speak volumes and I feel a pang of guilt, realizing that they are taken at the expense of all the unhappy people waiting in the cold.

Another half hour passes and the bus line now hosts twenty shivering souls. Likely, most of them are thinking, "If the line at this stop is so long, what about the people waiting at the stops before this one?" They probably realize that, after standing for so long in the cold, they will have to stand on a crowded, jerky bus or the bus could be full and may not stop at all.

I wonder why most people waiting there may not own a car: "Possibly too young, too old, too poor, can't drive, afraid to drive, or once ran someone down and vowed never to drive again."

My thoughts went to the millions of people around the world that were at that very moment waiting in extreme heat, freezing cold or torrential rain for a bus to come along.

My sense of guilt was heightened as I considered that I had a seventy-thousand-dollar car sitting outside - and two convertibles in the garage - and was in a warm and comfortable café watching unfortunate souls, some possibly developing frostbite. The very old or infirm may be experiencing severe fatigue and cramps and may not be able to stand or keep their balance much longer. It's still 22 degrees and they are all craning their necks in the direction of the bus.

Still no bus in sight.

At that moment in time, life for them is all about the bus that isn't coming and the incompetent public transportation system that has - once again - failed them in the worst weather. The old lady with the shrill voice has stopped talking to conserve the little energy she has. Each worry about something, like being late for a job or interview, a doctor's appointment they may miss, a rendezvous with a friend or family member.

I pack up my computer and exit the warm shop. I climb into my luxury SUV and pull away as some twenty-five people have no choice but to continue waiting or abort their plans. "Life is not fair," I think, as I drive past them and recite out loud a popular proverb, "We make plans and God laughs."

BREAK AWAY

It was a hot and oppressive August day in the big city. I stepped into my metallic-blue 1956 Olds 88 convertible, put the white top down – and headed into a dream.

The muggy air soon dissipated and became cool and refreshing as the city vanished behind me. Like leaving Sodom and Gomorrah, I never looked back until I was a safe distance from the concrete towers and bumper-to-bumper traffic. Now, with a clear head, I welcomed the lush green countryside and winding ribbons of black asphalt, seemingly rolled out moments earlier, just for me.

I arrived in the serene, lush Berkshire Mountains - a place I'd left behind in my youth and that I now knew longed to find me and me, it.

In the big city, dreams of escape are often disrupted by the piercing back-up beeps and putrid drippings of N.Y. garbage trucks, by the sweaty, garlic-breathed folk on subway trains, and the nasty, disgruntled people in the streets; there are distrusting souls in the marketplace closely guarding their valuables and loud, leaned-on horns of the angry and frustrated drivers, inching through traffic at a one-block-a-light pace. Overly dramatic sirens of emergency vehicles screech past beggars of every age, color and gender, and city folk all suited up, rush here and there to do 'important stuff' that tomorrow will be dismissed as unnecessary - if remembered at all.

On the bus, on the train, and on the park benches, the faces of strangers are hidden by the daily headlines: the latest scandal, the bombing yesterday far away, a local tenement fire that killed a family of five, the latest threats from North Korea, another presidential *faux pas*. They shout out about affairs of the rich and famous, the greed of the already rich, about human suffering from tragic 'acts of God' - tornadoes, hurricanes, earthquakes, floods, forest fires - and the sexiest men and women to walk the planet.

In the countryside, the streets, houses, mountains and general store have not changed much in fifty years. I discover that here there are (mostly) people that do not live in constant pain, discomfort, anguish, fear, and frustration. They are not constantly bombarded by the fear of crime, the malaise of discontent, of ignorance and downright stupidity. There are no ugly, grey, high-rise buildings, each window filled with a different story of life in the naked city.

Now I live in a log house on an unpaved road, high on a mountain. I know peace, nature and wholesome values that are not steeped in material wealth or depressing poverty.

Now I can cut wood and flowers, plant carrots and tomatoes, pledge allegiance, listen to folk music and birds sing, and have no fear of the darkness.

And, as Thoreau wrote in *Walden Pond*, sometimes we need to "plant turnips and act silly."

HEY, JEW!

"Fredrick, now that you suspect that one or both of your boys are not yours, what are you going to do about it?"

Frederick responds, "They both look like me, so I will just leave it alone for the moment."

I knew all about Giulia, the young and beautiful Italian woman forty years Fredrick's junior, who was his server on several occasions in a fancy restaurant in Rome. He asked her out one day and she - nearly broke and looking for a sugar daddy - accepted. He wined and dined Giulia each time he was in Rome, always leaving her some cash, even though she never actually asked for money.

Yes, they did go to his hotel room and eventually she invited him to her small flat in the Rome ghetto. Once he saw the area she lived in, he suggested that they only stay at his hotel when he was in town, and Giulia was good with that. Eventually, he set her up in an expensive chalet he purchased in a gated community on the Amalfi coast.

Fredrick is now 90. He is still in good health. He has signed over the chalet to Giulia and his two sons. He has a good relationship with Giulia, probably because she is now older and likely no longer fooling around with other men. He sent his boys to top universities - one lives in Madrid and one in Paris - and they come to visit their father often in New York City.

He no longer plays tennis, but has not given up his passion for the game and is riveted to the TV during the U.S. Open; he always has a prime seat at the U.S. Open at Flushing Meadows and rarely misses a match. He is still a ladies' man but now, to his extreme embarrassment, Viagra doesn't always work. He still buys custom-made shirts and suits, still has a passion for silk hosiery and good steak and, yes, still lives the good life as best a ninety-year-old man can.

Fredrick is a Jew who was smart - and lucky - enough to have escaped from Poland at the start of the Nazi occupation. He left with a small bag holding toiletries and a change of underwear; 100 U.S. dollars was hidden in the underwear.

At the final checkpoint leaving Polish territory, he presented his passport to the SS guard, looking him squarely in the face without expression. He was asked some rudimentary questions and answered each one without hesitation. He had practiced his answers, his facial expressions and voice modulation for several weeks in preparation for his moment of escape.

"Why are you traveling?" the guard asked 'Henrik' in a soft, almost-friendly voice, probably to catch him off guard. Henrik said that he was visiting his cousin for a few days. He had an address, but was not asked for it. Noting his common Polish (non-Jewish) name, the officer did not question his papers, and waved him through the checkpoint. The guard must have had second thoughts, because when Henrik was thirty yards from freedom, he yelled out in Polish, "Hey, Jew!", something most Jews may have had a knee jerk reaction to. In that fateful split second, when he thought his heart would stop, when he forced his legs not to hesitate and his mind to ignore the guard, he kept walking and saved his life. Had he responded at all, he would have been shot before he reached freedom. When he passed through Freedom's

Gate, he looked back and saw the guard's rifle still pointing in his direction.

He told me one day that those thirty meters, walking away from that Nazi to freedom, were the longest and most terrifying moments of his life; they would return in his nightmares, when he would wake shaking and soaked in sweat. When fully conscious, he realizes it's another nightmare and that he is still alive. And even though he gave up on religion when all his family and friends perished in the death camps, he thanks God for his luck and quick thinking that fateful moment seventy years ago.

CARLITA'S CURVES

Carlita's lightning-quick sense of humor and classic beauty set her apart from most of the women at the ritzy country club cocktail party.

By fifteen, Carlita knew that her large cobalt blue eyes were one of her secret weapons, and when she intentionally opened them really wide, she could get what she wanted from any man, her daddy included.

By eighteen, she had blossomed into a beautiful woman with an exquisite figure, including a male-magnet cleavage. Her captivating beauty coupled with extraordinary intelligence, uncanny common sense, finishing school grace, a superb sense of humor, and elegant composure and charm, drew men in like a Venus flytrap.

She had the unique ability to listen attentively to more than one conversation at a time and, regardless of distractions, return and repeat each pursuer's last sentence, acknowledging each man with wide-eyed, feigned interest. With uncanny wit, she would turn the pursuer's questions around, usually throwing him off guard - her favorite thing.

Carlos was single and clearly a fine catch, preferring Jewish women at least ten years his junior. A self-made millionaire, he had immigrated to Venezuela with his parents when he was five. His father - a tailor by trade - came at the invitation of his uncle, who had departed Cuba some years before. Having seen the political unrest in Cuba, Carlos's uncle realized that there was little future for them under the oppressive Batista dictatorship. Batista's goons had already stolen much of their wealth and he realized that it would likely be worse if Castro and his band of communist bandits managed to overthrow Batista - which we know is exactly what happened.

Impish, charismatic, well known (and very well liked), Carlos perused the glamorous crowd to see if any of his friends had arrived; and that's when he spied and became mesmerized by Carlita's curves.

He stopped here and there for friendly banter, moving slowly and inconspicuously towards the beautiful, intriguing new addition to his highbrow social scene. Some at the gathering had not seen Carlos since the tragic death of his young wife and - with genuine, heartfelt sincerity - stopped him and quietly offered their condolences.

As he approached Carlita, she felt his presence, turned and looked down at him, he being a good foot shorter than her. She smiled, held her stare for a few seconds longer than necessary and turned back to chat with the other attractive young suitors surrounding her. She had no interest in Carlos, but it was her way to play. The coy little flirt made eye contact with Carlos from time to time, just to keep him tethered. She loved the attention and the more men hanging around her, the greater the adrenalin rush that fueled her narcissistic psyche.

In a brief moment of silence, while listening carefully to the conversation, Carlos jumped in with a witty retort – rewarded with a belly laugh from all. One by one the men moved on to freshen their drinks and play the field, so when only Carlos remained, he wasted no time in inviting her to a party at his home. She intentionally showed interest for a moment, opening her eyes wide, teasing him with a big smile. She then breathed in deeply, knowing that it would raise her breasts and accentuate her cleavage, and slowly exhaled exclaiming, "Oh, I'm so sorry, Rafael, I forgot. I have other plans for that evening. Perhaps some other time?" Intuitively he knew that she had no intention of 'another time' and was just being a little bitch. And, of course, she knew that he knew and accepted that she had no intention of coming to his party; this guy that was a foot shorter, not very attractive, and far too old.

Carlita was an attorney, so Carlos easily acquired her phone number from the Yellow Pages. After several attempts, she took his call and - to his surprise and delight - agreed to meet him for a drink. By then, she had forgotten that he was a foot shorter and quite a bit older, but she liked his voice and wanted to network and, perhaps, because he had influence, he could recommend her professional services to some of his wealthy business friends.

He knew Carlita was an uphill challenge with little prospect of success, but 'charm' was his middle name. He always liked a challenge and wanted to add her to his growing stable of beautiful women he had and intended to bed.

He made no advances at first - just a casual lunch or drinks at the club. Always the gentleman, he was there to open the door, light her cigarette, push in her chair, help her on with her jacket, or give her his if she had a chill. Other than a light touch to her shoulder, he never made physical contact. After some time, Carlita - who knew his reputation - started to wonder why he asked for not as much as a kiss on the cheek or a serious dinner date; and why each time they parted, he ceremoniously kissed her hand, offering only a promise to call her again.

Weeks passed between calls, which precipitated Carlita's curiosity and growing interest in this impish, charismatic man. As time passed, she began to see past his height and less-than-attractive face; the strong smell of the unlit Cuban cigar he always had perched between his lips became a subconscious aphrodisiac. She had a handful of tall, virile, good-looking and wealthy suitors, but slowly she fell in love with Carlos' charm. His amazing sense of humor kept her laughing and in good spirits; his worldly ways, his penchant for detail, his plethora of interesting stories, and his lust for life made her feel more alive than any other man she had ever dated. As time went by, he reeled her into intimacy, but she had somehow turned the tables and reeled him into a proposal of marriage.

It was a fairytale society wedding and she moved into the magnificent home that he had built for his first wife, who had died in the house. A year later, Carlita gave birth to a son and they anticipated a long, happy-ever-after together.

I knew Carlos for many, many years and way after his divorce from Carlita. When the honeymoon year was over, he regressed to his philandering ways. She knew it, but she loved him deeply and, for a long, painful period, couldn't get up the courage to call it quits. At social events, she quickly became acutely aware of ill-mannered, *entitled* women who purposely stared at her, whispering and giggling about her in her presence.

She was ripe for an affair of her own and fell in love with a tall, handsome attorney. Only then did she find the strength to leave him. Her love for Carlos had died; he had killed it day by painful day with his many indiscriminate, selfish and devastating acts of betrayal.

Carlos was a hopeless romantic and no matter where I bumped into him traveling the world, he had a beautiful woman on his arm and under his spell. However, time passed and his health declined; his face went from impish to grotesque, and his body became heavy and twisted. He dragged himself around, first with a cane and then with a walker.

Now, even his charm and money were not enough to attract and hold onto young beauties, and he settled for a different kind of woman: one who would be content to share his money and his lifestyle, In return for a new dress, a trip to Paris, she would take care of him.

Through most of his adult life, people flocked to Carlos. He had hundreds of friends, and his charm and sense of humor attracted men and women alike. He had impressive influence and was respected in his wealthy community. He knew many important politicians and generals, and - where others needed money to extract special favors - Carlos could get most anything he wanted through charm alone.

I admired Carlos, enjoyed the time I spent with him and was very sad to hear about his passing. This was a man that lived every day to the full and I sometimes ponder… in the winter of his life, as his time to leave was coming close, having the opportunity to do it over, would he have embraced Carlita as his life partner and could he have been true to her alone?

I don't think it was his nature to be faithful or to be with just one woman and, as a self-made millionaire son of a tailor, I suspect he had no regrets and a big smile on his face as he departed.

As the saying goes: "He did it his way."

BATTERY LIFE

Damn my alarm - it's 6 already – what's the weather – check phone –

battery 88% - should take me through the day - I hope - I'll take the backup battery just in case - that will definitely take me through the day – I should have plugged it in last night - did I send the check for my electric bill on time - will my lights still go on when I get home tonight – what do they care that we cannot live without electricity – hey, it's only money they care about and not service - did Joan really mean what she said about my wrinkles or was she just being mean - or both - is she having an affair - I think so - what is *really* on her mind - I should look for another job - my boss is an ass - he has no idea how much work I do - maybe I should just change careers - this job isn't so enjoyable any more - check Facebook –

battery 76% - wish I could plug this in somewhere - damn, forgot the backup *and* the charger - why does that woman let her cigarette smoke blow towards her kid in the stroller - when the kid starts to cough and turns green, will she understand that it's from her cigarettes - smokers are selfish – out to lunch – addicted – can't help themselves - hold that elevator, mister - how inconsiderate - it would have only held him up a few seconds - I know he saw me - now I have to wait for four or five freakin' minutes for the next one and then I'll be late - again - I could lose my job - better work a little faster or stay late to catch up - maybe the guy was late for work also – he DID see me, I'm sure - check Instagram –

battery 71% - getting hungry – text Jane to remind her about lunch - sometimes she gets busy and forgets - this piece of fish is just not worth what they are charging – why did they even bother giving me such a small potato - what is that - could someone have sneezed on my food – there are so many airborne germs - we should be like the Japanese and wear a face mask when sick - they are so much more considerate - I hope my mother didn't fall and is now lying on the cold kitchen floor - maybe can't get up - if only I could get her to wear that alert thing - she is so independent - I better call her now – just in case

battery 71% - ah, battery good - it's selfish because us kids worry – no one answers - where the hell am I going to get the money for the kids' school trip - how will I tell them that they can't go if I can't find the money - could I ask the school if there is some kind public assistance that will pay this time - I think that my biggest client is thinking of switching suppliers – I'll have her neighbor check on her – text her - that would hurt my job performance - my company's fault - always delivering late - well then my other customers could find out and follow - what would I do without that damn paycheck and health insurance – I don't have enough savings to live on for too long - let me check Twitter –

battery 68% - Good - Mom was with her - why does this phone have such bad battery life - is there some app running all the time - is there a virus - these shoes are killing me - why don't they make them with better arches – they cost enough - is Peggy pregnant – she's been acting odd lately and not feeling well in the morning - I will ask her tonight if there is anything I should know - maybe I shouldn't ask - she is so damn independent – like me - my train delayed - was there an accident - it could be a few minutes or an hour – better check my emails –

battery 60% - should I call home and tell them I may be delayed - better wait a few minutes - I think I have enough battery to play a few games – just relax a bit –

battery 58% - this fruit seems a bit soft - hope I don't bite into a worm – gross - this train is driving me crazy – too cold - too hot - too muggy - too noisy - stop and go - stop and go - screeching wheels - nothing I can do about it - getting close - where did I park this morning in my usual rush - check car locator –

battery 57% - hope this stupid car starts – I think I'm getting bad gas mileage - maybe I should buy a more efficient car - is it worth changing cars now because that will cost more than the gas - why doesn't our government do something about gas prices - is that my phone - that's Elsa – I won't answer - she's too long-winded - need to save my battery - where is the car charger -

battery 56% - damn and it's already 5 PM - is that a mosquito bite on my neck or a deer tick - I could get Lyme - Frank got Lyme that way - almost killed him - they say to let the battery run out and then charge it - is that an urban myth - are my love handles growing - is this a gas pain or am I having a heart attack - shit - is that a pain in my arm - my heart - my imagination - damm city stress – how's my battery -

battery 55% - I could faint at the wheel - did Jack take my charger wire - why doesn't he ever take my side – this red light is ridiculous – so long - hmm - looks like that woman driving the Jag had her boobs fixed - so out of proportion - they are too high - wonder what her story is – a little anxiety - what's wrong with me - think I need a Caribbean getaway -

I have to stop listening to the news - so depressing - need to call Sue -

battery 52% - damn - how did I get sand in my shoes - haven't been to the beach since Sunday - my kid must have borrowed these shoes again - let me see if I have any messages -

battery 49% - no messages – that's odd - that motorcycle makes so much damn noise - there should be a law - need more toilet paper - it's terrible to run out on the can - I should remember always to check first - especially if I have no tissues - if she doesn't get better marks she may not graduate - all that time and money down the drain - did the dry cleaner shrink this - it fit me last month - I think - what time is it -

battery 49% - later than I thought - great, no battery loss - what would it be like making love on that beach - he's too damn practical and hates sand - are the girls there yet - there they are - Flo looks terrible - this should perk me up - I've been drinking too many of those sugar-laden drinks - oh well, I'll have the salad - are those girls lesbians over there holding hands - could I be a latent lesbian - that rhymes - latent lesbian – those street Rolexes look good - what if it stops working tomorrow - it's a thirty buck risk – no big deal - love handles - have to work out more but no time - in just a week I will be a year older - see if Sue sent me a text - not yet -

battery 46% - stay off the damn phone, girl - always checking - it's addicting - how great it would be to be on a beautiful white sandy beach right now and not with chattering ladies - stupid conversations - they're getting on my nerves - oh that guy looks like my dad - my dad is such a good guy - I may be his favorite - I am really good to him - this mirror makes me look fat - see if my little girl called –

maybe dad can fund the kids trip – hell with the kids, send me to the Caribbean - I wonder if she's home yet - check text -

battery 44% - damn battery - why am I so tired - maybe I have cancer - is there another side - heaven and hell - where did those words come from anyway - let me check to see if I have cancer symptoms - Wikipedia - nothing definitive - vague - guess I'm okay - better get back in the conversation - check text -

battery 40% - I need to get a trim - add a little color to the roots - was this made with child labor - it's so cheap – best that I don't know because I want it – hmm, Bangladesh – where the hell is that anyway - what will happen if we have a flood - it could happen - those poor people that lost everything in that tsunami - haven't checked email in an hour - see what the weather is tomorrow -

battery 38% hmm, I'll check it later - what are those people staring at - do I know them - they must think I'm a celebrity or something - there are a few famous people that look like me - I really can't afford to lose my job - must be nice not to look at price tags - wonder what Oprah sees in front of the mirror naked - should I tell my daughter to use protection – did she text me yet -

battery 33% - nothing yet - this checkout clerk is so nice - why can't they all be like this - I guess many people take their problems to work - I try not to but some days it's hard - I have so much trouble going to work on Monday - it's the job - I missed Frank's call –

battery 26% - uh, this phone's rapidly dying - will the nursery take back that dying bush from last fall – I've got to pee - the conversation is stupid - just say not feeling well and make a quick exit – not hungry anyway- should have plugged in at the restaurant –

battery 24% - that oil change light is so annoying - ok car - I'll change it when I have time - I'm sure the oil is just fine - why don't they clean up this garbage in the street - we pay so much in taxes - these radio commercials are so annoying - so repetitive and insulting -I better tell Fran that her check bounced - should I tell her that I got charged twenty five bucks - those bank charges are such a rip off - banks - shit - don't say anything - just take cash from her now - get detergent and call Sam the plumber - again - nice guy but so unreliable - what a rat race this is - is that pigeon sick – it's head looks all pecked up - why is it allowed to fly onto those picnic tables - they carry disease - what about a dog - always wanted a dog but it must be small so I don't have to pick up too much poop - big commitment - forget it for now - our hamster is good enough for now - but dogs are such good companions - all sizes and shapes - check the weather for tonight -

battery 20% -will I make it home on 20% - what does that person eat to look like that - who am I to judge – can't seem to get going today - no energy - I need a power nap - my watch stopped - battery I guess - I'll check my phone –

battery 14% - no way - it was just 6 o'clock! - why are people moving away - do my pits smell? - I hear that Asians don't sweat - that can't be true - bottled water is such a rip off - tap water is just fine for me - so much plastic - what is she knitting - baby stuff - is she pregnant –overweight - fat - maybe it's for a good friend or her sister - who cares – I need some cold water now - I'll get a bottle from here - what a hypocrite I am - but I'm thirsty and there's no fountain around - get some chips, too – damn, left my wallet in the office – no problem - pay with apple pay-

battery 2% better hurry, I'm next - **damn, screen went black** - oh no – can't pay - and I already opened the water and chips - the cashier gal will understand - probably sees this happen every day - I hope she will trust me till tomorrow -

Gee, what a lonely, helpless feeling - being alone and vulnerable like this without a phone for another twenty minutes – I better not forget the backup battery again.

BUS PASS

When my dad passed, I had the job of rummaging through the old shed behind his house containing wooden boxes sealed and stored for generations. As I pried off the top of each, I discovered a trove of family memorabilia going back to the 1890s. The oldest piece was a faded black and white photo of my grandfather in a Latvian uniform with a still-visible comment in the bottom border: *Boer War, South Africa, 1897.*

I also came across my worn and faded yellow bus pass, valid for the second half of the 1957 school year. Without much thought, I tossed it in the trash, along with many other things I had no connection to. When I was almost finished with the project, something beckoned me to retrieve the bus pass and, when I held it again, I felt a need to keep it; I slipped it into an unused slot in my wallet.

Each time I changed wallets, the fragile and ragged bus pass was carefully moved to its new home. After some years I had it laminated, because it was deteriorating and I was at that point keeping it both as a talisman and a reminder of my youth.

Some twenty-five years later, I drove through the neighborhood where I grew up and noticed with amusement that the bus stop where I had waited to go to school each morning was still in the same location. The neighborhood had changed dramatically and now only the post office and a few other shops survived. My father's fabric and custom slipcover draperies shop was now a busy pizzeria.

It was an October day in 1982. The air smelled just as I remembered it in my youth, bringing back a flood of teen memories. My knee-jerk impulse was to park my car, which I did, and for strictly nostalgic reasons, I ambled over to the bus stop. The bus had just pulled in and the passengers were exiting. This was the last stop on the bus route, having traveled twenty-one miles from the Jamaica subway station to the last stop at Springfield and Horace Harding Boulevards in Bayside, Queens.

I watched the traffic whizz by, as I often did as a kid. I found myself reminiscing about the carefree, sometimes awkward, but mostly happy days of my youth. I had a flashback of a frigid day in my short leather jacket and white tee shirt, holding a cigarette cuffed in the palm of my hand, engaging the girls, making small talk with my pals and, of course, always following the guys' code of conduct: no matter what, *always look and act cool.*

The bus gave a long and loud hiss as the driver released the air from the brakes and exited the bus, pulling the door partially closed behind him. He ran into a little luncheonette a few feet away and, minutes later, exited with a pack of cigarettes and a cup of coffee. He immediately lit up and, without a moment to spare, inhaled deeply. With the smoke still in his lungs, he took several large gulps of coffee, exhaled, flicked off the lit end of the cigarette and carefully pushed it back into the pack to continue his routine later.

School started at eight-thirty and it was now nine. Without thinking, I reached for my wallet, pulled out my bus pass and climbed onto the bus. I looked up and I thought, "It's Fred, the regular driver on this route twenty-five years ago. How is this possible?"

"You're late again, sonny-boy," he said playfully, scolding me with his finger as I boarded the bus.

"What the hell is going on here?" I thought. "This guy hasn't aged a day."

Fred remembered me. He didn't look at my bus pass, just waved me in. "No horsing around, kid," he said in his familiar raspy voice as I passed him and grunted in agreement. I walked slowly to the back of the bus where the boys always sat to be boisterous and push the envelope of bad behavior – and, of course, to smoke.

As I made my way down the aisle, the modern, industrial-strength velvet seating morphed suddenly into the molded pink plastic seats of my youth. I shook my head back and forth several times in disbelief and to clear my head. The posters above the windows slowly faded from current ads and returned to vintage cigarette ads - one was a brand that no longer existed. Each was promoted by a celebrity hawking the 'health and relaxation benefits of their cigarettes'; most who, incidentally, had since died from lung cancer.

An old poster of the Doublemint chewing gum twins appeared above me in the panels over the seats, along with Tide and Ivory Snow posters with soap opera stars of yester-year promoting their washday products. There was an ad for the all-new, soon-to-be-available 1957 Chevy, with a smiling, clean-cut young man behind the wheel exuding satisfaction with an ear-to-ear grin, his slim, basic-issue, drably-dressed wife in the passenger seat, looking with great reverence at her man. The kids were jumping around in the back - before seat belts, of course - their hands in the air as if they were traveling 100 miles an hour. There were advertisements for secretarial schools teaching shorthand -

both Pitman and Gregg - and employment agencies guaranteeing everyone a great-paying job with a future.

I was standing holding onto the pole near the back exit of the bus when it came to an abrupt stop at the school. It was like days of old, as I catapulted around the pole and - with the same forward motion - jumped down the two steps, pushed the back door open and jumped off. When I looked down, I noticed that my beer belly was gone and I could see my fifteen-year-old reflection on the bus door as it pulled away.

I walked into the school as students were moving to their Period 2 classrooms. The five-minute warning bell sounded and I remembered that, for me, Period 2 was woodworking shop at the end of the hall on the first floor. Our teacher - Mr. Johannsson - was standing, arms crossed, waiting for the remainder of the students to trickle in. He was a tall Scandinavian gentleman with a full head of grey hair. His big concern always and understandably was safety around the power tools. If you fooled around or got careless, he would come up behind you and put one of his huge hands on your shoulder and squeeze it just enough to send his message.

When I entered the room, I expected him to be surprised to see me, but I forgot that it was just another school day in 1957. When all the boys had settled in on their high metal stools, he explained the day's woodworking project. I loved that class. I took after my dad and always enjoyed working with my hands, building useful stuff.

I went through my other morning classes, saw all of my old friends including the girl I had a crush on back then - a beautiful brunette with a uniquely twisted double ponytail. Then, on to the lunchroom, where I shared a table with some of my buddies. Talk was the same stuff each day: girls, sports, cars, teachers, the hot female gym teacher and rumors about her affair with the men's gym teacher. Actually, it was true; their contracts were not renewed the following year because they were married to other people.

I put my hand in my pocket for some change and realized that the bus pass was missing. Frantically, I looked in my wallet and in all my pockets. It was gone for sure and I knew the time warp - or whatever it was I was in - would soon thrust me back to 1982. I could see things were already changing, especially the size of my stomach and the wrinkles on my hands.

I walked rapidly to an exit where a familiar guard was stationed. I waved to him and said, "Hi Harold!" as I left, but he could no longer see or hear me.

Then I was back at the bus stop as my older self. The bus that arrived was a modern one with nice fabric seats, ads for 1983 cars, stereophonic music systems, electric typewriters, modern washing machines, and color TVs.

I knew that no one would believe my strange experience so, until now, I've not shared it with a soul. But I'm quite certain that, for a brief few hours, I defied time when my bus pass was my ticket into my past.

My bus pass stayed in 1957 where it belonged and would finally be tossed into the trash, this time for good.

I LOVED THE MAN

When we worked together, it was a symbiotic, magical and unique 'concert of two'. There was an uncanny understanding between us that I can describe best as a *business ballet* - well-choreographed by logic, intuitive behavior, and a respect for one another's moves. Even, I'm sure at times, an element of mental telepathy.

We shared an amazing synergy. He would say 'do', or 'get' or 'take note' and, without hesitation, I would comply. With his broken English accent, facial expressions and hand gestures, he would tell me what he wanted and like an obedient soldier, willing and without hesitation, I would carry out his wishes.

It was business and there was a healthy profit in it for me, but that only scratched the surface of our relationship. We worked together for many years and, intuitively, I knew what he wanted. He was fun to be with, had a great sense of humor and - despite being a conservative Sephardic Jew from Morocco - he was, in my humble opinion, a free spirit of a man. Different from most I had met in my life.

He was a big man and a few years my senior. I, like many, was in awe of his confidence and ability to make the right choices most of the time. He was also *simpatico*, which is hard to translate but loosely means 'engaging, charming, likable, sympathetic, and pleasant'. When we went to see his clients in Caracas, it was akin to someone visiting family. Customers smiled when he arrived, stopped what they were doing - even if they were busy - and listened to what he had to say.

He remembered the names of his clients' children and spouses and their family issues of the moment. Kindness, empathy, and understanding were his calling cards. He could also sell you the Brooklyn Bridge, but if you bought it, he delivered it, and if he said it would be good, it usually was.

Most of his clients knew him from the Jewish community, but he also sold to the Arab and Christian clothing manufacturers and - as far as I could tell - they all liked him and held him in the highest regard. They knew that Hillel could be trusted, was always right on the cutting edge of fashion, and if he had something in his hand to show you, you should probably buy some.

Because he appeared larger than life, when he passed on suddenly, it was hard for family, friends, and business associates to believe, accept and get their head around the news. I am one who still can't quite get my head around his premature and sudden passing.

I often think of my times with him in the Caracas garment center, in the restaurants, at his home, to which I was invited often and considered family. I think of him in New York, running non-stop from one textile supplier to the next, and attending fashion trade shows looking for the latest trends. He would see a new fabric, look at me and, within a few days, we would be purchasing exactly what he had seen.

I think of the amazing weddings he made for his two children and the guests that arrived from around the world, who - for days before the wedding - were treated to endless tours, lunches, and dinners; and to discover, when we checked out of the five-star hotel, that even the hotel tab was paid for by him!

Hillel gave me a card with a drawing of a Rabbi for good luck and told me to always keep it with me. It's worn and tattered and, to this day, resides in my wallet - not so much for luck, but to remember and honor Hillel, the man I love, respect and miss.

In my home, among the framed pictures of my family is a picture of Hillel. He was - and still is - family.

FLANKEN MEMORIES

Flanken. The word flows easily through my lips and triggers many childhood memories. If you are Jewish and your family roots are from Europe, chances are you can conjure up the smell and taste of this delicacy.

If you've never heard of flanken, it's a wonderful, old-world preparation of short ribs, seasoned with horseradish and served on a generous portion of wide egg noodles and brown gravy from the broth. Cooked and seasoned properly, you will never tire of this melt-in-your-mouth delicacy.

Growing up, I lived with my grandparents from time to time; first as a teenager for a year and then again after my divorce until I was drafted. Rumor has it that I was Grandma's favorite. My room in my grandparents' house was in the finished attic, just above the kitchen. In the summer, the sun would beat down on the roof and - because there was no air conditioning - my room was like an oven by 10 am.

My grandmother always started cooking the flanken early on a Sunday morning. The process of cooking in a pressure cooker created a terribly nauseating smell that wafted up the stairs and into my sleeping nostrils. This most unpleasant smell would wake me from my Saturday-night, alcohol-induced hangover and - soaked in perspiration and lethargic from the unbearable heat of the rising sun - I would roll out of bed and make my way downstairs.

While the flanken was cooking, my grandmother would remove the plastic seat covers from the couch and chairs in the living room. The immediate family was never allowed in the living room; it was used strictly to impress friends and distant relatives.

Julia, my grandmother, had lots of energy, especially when cooking for the extended family. It was usually my grandmother's side of the family who would arrive about noon, but sometimes my grandfather's relatives from Czechoslovakia - holocaust survivors - would make the tedious, two-hour train and bus trip from the Bronx.

My sister Bev, our cousin Terry and I always looked forward to these family get-togethers at Grandma's. The food was amazing, and my uncles Paul and Benny were very funny and loved to entertain the kids. Sometimes, when this group got together, male egos clashed creating spirited arguments over the most mundane of subjects.

When a shouting match broke out, first my grandmother tried to calm the men down and, when she couldn't, my grandfather's temper kicked in. He would start screaming at everyone in Hungarian, which no one else understood. By the time he ran out of steam, the arguing had stopped and we all commenced eating. Usually, the arguments were about ridiculous things like the shortest route to Brooklyn or the best gas to use for the new model cars, and each of the men - my father excluded - would get into the argument. It was a male ego thing, but my father could care less and was very likely already taking a nap in the den.

My grandmother was born in America from German stock and was the self-proclaimed matriarch of the family - a role she handled with great diplomacy. Most of the time.

My grandfather, Aaron, was trained by my grandmother to do nothing around the house, which he excelled at. His six-day-a-week routine consisted of: shave, shower, dress, buy newspaper, read paper on subway to Manhattan, get breakfast, walk to his valet laundry, greet customers, fold and pack the clean clothing in boxes, count cash at day's end, and bring some money to the bank at closing.

On Thursdays, he would play pinochle with friends and bring home the winnings in his socks. He almost always won. Behind my grandfather's legitimate 'don't know how to use a can opener or open a quart of milk' facade, he was a brilliant pinochle player. He won so often that this contributed substantially to the down payment on their first home in Queens - liberation from the treeless brick-and-concrete crowded tenements in the Bronx.

Occasionally, some of us challenged him to a game of gin rummy. He always had a poker face when he played and, just when one of us thought we were about to win, he showed his amazing hand. We never understood how he did it, but I think he was able to remember all the cards we picked up and dropped. He may have been just a laundryman - not rocket science - but he was a whizz with numbers and cards. My grandmother always prodded him ("let the children win once in a while"), but he just couldn't do it. He could not cheat like that.

Owning a home was a big deal back then. Everyone else in the family either lived in a rented high-rise apartment in the Bronx or a garden apartment co-op in Queens. My grandmother was a first-rate, Jewish status seeker and reveled in the fact that she was the only one in the family with her own house, her own piece of land, her own garden, her own rose arbor in the front of the house, and her own grape arbor in the back.

It was a small house with one bedroom, one bathroom, a den, a living room, a kitchen and an unfinished attic, which was eventually turned into my bedroom. In the 1950s, the purchase price was a mere $19,990. There was no basement and the house had radiant heating in the floor (it felt so good in the winter), a decent-size front yard and a respectable backyard big enough for an enclosed patio, a 10 x 10 slab of concrete for table, chairs and an umbrella.

When my grandparents first moved into the house, the streets were not paved and the bulldozers had not arrived yet to clear the wooded area across the street for the next row of little houses. I dug out a few small maple seedlings from the woods and replanted one in the front yard and one in the back.

There were many wonderful Sundays at Grandma's. It was the American dream-come-true and we were fortunate enough to be a part of it - in part through my grandmother's daily quest to make sure her family had the very best of everything.

I'm sure that the Great Depression and the Second World War left lasting emotional scars on anyone old enough to have lived through them. People like my grandmother overcompensated, wanting to be sure that her children and grandchildren had the opportunity for a good life.

At some point, my grandmother decided to take the outdoor furniture off the concrete deck in the back of the house and place it under the grape arbor, which now had sprawling, shady vines, and green wine grapes in the summer. She installed the first above-ground pool in the neighborhood on the concrete slab. I arrived home from work one day and was overwhelmed by the size and height of the pool. I couldn't wait to change, jump in and get out of the oppressive July heat. What luxury!

My grandparents' legacy was more than flanken memories. It was that rich experience of growing up in America when life was simple, when gas was twenty-five cents a gallon, and when we were innocent children.

Thanks, Grandma. And you too, Grandpa.

CLASSIC LIZARD

"Reservations, gentlemen?" Francisco the maître d' inquires softly with a less-than-genuine well-practiced smile, tilting his head to the right and waiting for a response.

"Franklin is the name."

Francisco, holding a stubby pencil, runs his crooked arthritic forefinger down the reservation list, whispering to himself, "Franklin, Franklin." As he finds it and crosses it out, he smiles again and, with a theatrical flourish of his hand, turns the gentlemen over to an attractive brunette for seating, saying, "Have an enjoyable lunch. Thank you for joining us."

Sheila takes the men to a table next to a large group of well-dressed 'suits', even though the dining room is conspicuously empty.

"We would prefer something quieter," requests one of the men.

Sheila responds curtly, cutting him off and informing him with an air of authority, "Sorry, the other stations are now closed for lunch."

The men look at each other with surprise and then back at Sheila, manifesting their displeasure. She picks up their vibes, clears her throat, lowers her head and - in a much kinder voice - responds, "Please give me a moment, gentlemen. I will speak to the maître d'," as she spins around on her spiked heels and disappears.

This is Sheila's second day on the job. For the past five years, she's alternated the breakfast and lunch shift at a diner on the shabby side of town, where standard fare is weak coffee, deep-fried everything, brash treatment by the customers - especially to the young, good-looking women serving - and lousy, often non-existent tips. Now, with perspiration tickling her ribs and tummy, she muses, "I need to move up in the world and I need to change my approach, 'cause these people don't take any crap, and really - for what they're payin' for pasta - can't say I blame 'em."

As the two gentlemen wait for Sheila's return, one quietly elbows the other, making him aware of a striking blond looking their way from the table of suits. Her navy blazer is open, revealing a deep cleavage. The men smile at each other and then back at her. She is clearly enjoying the attention of these two handsome gentlemen.

Sheila returns and now, with a more cheerful voice and a bit of a flirty smile, informs them: "Gentlemen, the maître d' said you can sit *anywhere* you like." The two men pick a table, sit down and, in unison, flare open their starched white napkins, as Sheila hands them their menus. The tension in the back of her neck dissolves once she senses that the men are now smiling at her and aren't holding a grudge.

Sheila walks away and, with little to do now, goes outside for a quick smoke. "Maybe I'll snag one of these good-lookin' rich guys and I won't need to carry a tray or maybe work at all," she fantasizes. "I've got the youth and sex appeal to attract any of these suits. Lots of rich men come into ritzy places like this and some fall for hot chicks like me. It's time for a family, time for some luxury in my life." She thinks about Julia Roberts and Richard Gere in *Pretty Woman*. "That could be me if I play my cards right - but I would never take money for sex." She ponders, "I need to work on my vocabulary, learn lots of educated words, and speak only with a *soft voice*."

She returns shortly after their food and drinks are served and asks if everything is satisfactory. She hesitates for a brief moment; she clearly wants to say more but feels a bit apprehensive. She starts to leave, but turns back and blurts out: "I just started this job. It's my second day, and I apologize for not being as accommodating as I could have been."

The two men are pleasantly surprised and somewhat amused by her naive and genuine sincerity. They both had similar thoughts - that she knew who they *really* were and that was why she was being so nice. But, in fact, she didn't.

Jeff speaks first: "That was very thoughtful, miss, and very much appreciated. We had a feeling that this may have been a new job for you. Good luck," he continues with an approving smile as he looks up into her beautiful brown eyes. He thinks to himself that she's a quick study, has common sense, and knows when to change direction.

When she walks away, Jeff says to Frank, "She stays. She may not have much class... yet, but she has humility and street smarts, and we can train her. She's got potential."

Frank adds, "And she's quite a looker to boot." Both share a quick, chauvinistic laugh at the woman's expense, as they toast to having secretly acquired the restaurant. "Look, Jeff, we've never owned a restaurant before, so we don't really know what's good or bad, right or wrong. But that gal did the right thing and I admire that," Frank says in a whisper, as they navigate their lunch, with an eye on the cleavage still drawing their attention from across the room.

When the bill comes, Jeff takes out his wallet and removes his black American Express card, a sure sign of wealth. Sheila has heard about the black card, but has never seen one – and she is also drawn to Jeff's unusual wallet. In the diner, almost every guy had a bulging and deformed old wallet, two inches thick, filled with ragged, dirty pieces of paper from the time of the flood, and some cash. But very few had credit cards.

"This guy's wallet is absolutely beautiful," she thinks to herself. "It's real classy and sophisticated." She stares at it conspicuously for several seconds too long. Jeff notices and asks her if there is something wrong. "No, no," she stutters and with complete sincerity blurts out, "I'm sorry to stare, but I've never seen such a beautiful wallet. Is it leather?"

Jeff smiles up at her. "It's lizard," he responds softly. "I'm glad you like it."

Sheila has never seen a lizard wallet and always thought that lizards were just slimy critters. She never dreamed that anyone would make a wallet from their skin. As she walks away, she smiles and thinks to herself, "I know I'm from the other side of the tracks, but I like these classy guys and I'm gonna learn a lot in this joint and snag me a rich one!"

The classic lizard wallet. It's elegant, wears well, and impresses all that see it - even a waitress who dropped out of high school at sixteen and works for tips and minimum wage. She may be possibly one of the few to escape the American Heartland's cycle of the poorly educated living from paycheck to paycheck, dreaming of wealth from one lottery and scratch ticket to the next. The lottery ticket - modern society's opiate for the poor - as each dreams of a chance to share in America's wealth.

With perseverance, hard work and a bit of luck, Sheila may break with her family's history of poverty and poor education. She may enter the world of the middle class - or perhaps even the wealthy - and climb on the American dream-train to reach the station called Success.

BUZZ OFF

Even a simple-minded fly like me knows that being trapped here means a certain, slow death.

I guess I can't help getting myself into situations I can't seem to 'fly' out of. And then when I'm trapped, my survival DNA just keeps me flying around and around and around, looking for a way out of a closet or a bathroom and, once, even a kid's toy box. I thought I had spied a possible mate in the toy box, but it turned out to be a plastic fly. By the time I discovered this - boom - a little boy slammed the toy box shut and I had to wait until the next morning to escape.

Today, I've gotten myself into a real pickle, so to speak. I'm trapped between a window and a screen in this big old house. I've visited the entire edge of the window frame dozens of times, looking for a small hole for me to squeeze through without injuring my wings. It's hopeless! I ask myself, "How in heaven did I get between the window and the screen to begin with?"

Since I have no other choice and nothing else to do, I just look in the same places over and over again. There are two deadly spider webs here with me, one spun on the bottom and the other at the top; which, of course, means that at least one or two spiders were here at different times and *somehow* found a way in and a way out. I don't mean to analyze this to death, but if they *knew* that it was almost impossible for flies, moths or other tasty morsels to get in, why did they bother spinning the webs in the first place?

Hmm, I think I've got it. Someone left the window open; the spider (or spiders) wandered in, not realizing that windows open and close; they spun their deadly traps and left looking for other places to spin their webs or check out some of their recent traps for tasty morsels. My guess is that when the spider(s) returned, the window had been closed so, disappointed, they moved on to spin somewhere less problematic.

Actually, that's more or less what happened to me. I was minding my own business, flying around tasting all the goodies in the kitchen, and I decided to leave for a bit of fresh air. I headed for the window since the door was now closed and – bam - I hit the screen. It knocked the air out of me and, when I came to, a human had closed the window. And here I am. Trapped. Really, really bad luck for me.

It's not like I'm a cat stuck in a tree where I can let out loud meows or a dog having fallen into a deep hole where I could bark like crazy. Even though my wings sound much like an annoying dive bomber, no one hears me in the house through the closed window. I bang and bang on the glass, but it's hopeless. If the folks in the house do hear me, they will purposely not open the window because they don't want me in the house, so they just leave me here to die or spray me with some chemical from the outside to quicken my demise - so they can then reopen the window.

Actually, I don't think there are many humans who *really* want to rescue a fly, except possibly an innocent child who is tall enough and strong enough to reach up and open the window.

I'm hungry. I don't think humans truly understand hunger as we do. They appear to always have an abundance of food around and are extremely protective of it, even though we eat very little. They use their big hands to shoo us away when we hover over or land on their food.

I'm much too quick for them, so they employ a doomsday weapon to kill us; a thing they call a fly swatter. It's deadly, moving at lightning speed, and many of my friends and family have succumbed to it. Splat! The humans cheer or scream: "Got ya!" and we are finished, unceremoniously brushed into a napkin and tossed into the toilet. We're often just stunned, but then we drown. Until now, we usually had a fighting chance, because we would need to land first before being swatted. Now, they've gotten the ultimate doomsday weapon: the electric zapper. It looks like a tennis racket. Humans push a button to electrify the grid and they cremate us in midair. How thoughtless.

Humans think we defecate each time we land on their food. That's downright silly! We land often because we are tired or inquisitive or hungry or spy a possible mate. I've heard that they also believe we cause plagues and spread disease. Flypedia, our insectnet resource indicates that we are in fact very clean; some of us are even sterile.

However, to be fair, we often land on human trash - or worse - trash filled with bacteria. On a *rare* occasion, we may then land on a mountain of soft, delicious mashed potatoes with a warm tasty volcano gravy center. We all love mashed potatoes and *love* the soft landing. So, don't blame us if we land for a quick snack and happen to have just arrived straight from your festering garbage bin.

We appreciate it when humans leave doors, windows and screens open to allow us to enter.

Oh, here comes a little boy and he's planning to sit right outside my window with his bagel and cream cheese (another delicacy many of us flies fancy). I'd give anything now to get a taste of that cream cheese and wash it down with that sweet lemonade he's now slurping. Not only am I hot and hungry but now I'm quite thirsty. Perhaps I can buzz around and bang myself on the screen to get his attention, so he will feel sorry for me and open the screen and set me free before he finishes with the bagel. Look, even if he doesn't feel sorry for me, perhaps he will be annoyed with the racket I'm making and just want to get rid of me. Fat chance... kids don't care about noise. I think they like it and the louder the better.

He's coming closer now. He's looking at me. He's gigantic - just look at the size of his eyes! It looks like I may be in luck and he will set me free. I'll head straight for the cream cheese and take a sip of that lemonade before he can make it back to the table.

Oh no, he's changed his mind! He's distracted by that little girl approaching the table. Please little boy, don't go, don't go, please!

What bad luck. They are holding hands and she's sharing his lemonade. I hear her say she wants to go for ice cream (I adore ice cream). No point in buzzing and banging around now, because I'm alone and need to conserve my energy. For sure, I will stay *far away* from those spider webs.

It's survival of the fittest and fastest here on Planet Earth. Just one fly in a million, a billion - to be swept away at the next spring cleaning.

FIRST AND LASTING IMPRESSIONS

My working career began at a large curtain company located on the corner of Fifth Avenue and Thirty-Third Street in Manhattan. The building was built in 1890 by Aaron Demarest, a manufacturer of high-end motor carriages, and was notably the first building in Manhattan to install an electric elevator. The dramatic three-story arched windows were designed to let in massive amounts of daylight, so wealthy buyers could inspect the beautiful and expensive carriages under natural light.

It was a chilly October morning in 1959 when I reported for my first day of work at the company. Waiting for my boss to get off the phone, I surveyed the office space and - while glancing out the window overlooking Fifth Avenue - saw two men in white uniforms navigating their way out of the Empire State Building through the morning crowd, carrying a stretcher with a body bag.

That was a memorable moment for me as I thought, "How unpredictable life is. Here one moment, gone the next." I realized that someone was likely now delivering the heartbreaking news to the deceased's family. I thought that, no matter how empathetically delivered, it would translate to the family as "your loved one will not be coming home for dinner tonight or any night; not ever, ever again."

I envisioned it to be an older gentleman, one who had worked for the same firm for many years and always arrived at the job early. Without warning or prior health problems, he'd had a massive heart attack and was found slumped over his desk by a coworker. The ambulance pulled away and *things returned to normal*; that was, for everyone but the man in the body bag and his family.

I found it hard to concentrate that first day on the job, because of the recurring image of the body bag and the thought that a person wakes up, brushes their teeth, takes a shower, has breakfast with their spouse or family, kisses them and says, "Have a great day", leaves for work, reads the paper on the train as he's done for a lifetime - and never suspects that this will be his last newspaper and that, in a few days, he will be in the obituary column of the same paper.

I was hired as a textile sample clerk, which I soon discovered was a non-specific description for a 'gofer' and I would actually be performing all sorts of odd jobs around the office.

A week before starting the job, I visited an employment agency and, after they interviewed me, they gave me a dozen four-by-four inch mimeographed placement cards, each with a company name, contact person, phone number and address of a potential employer. When the young woman handed me the contact cards, she pointed out in a soft and serious voice, "Call this one last, because they haven't hired anyone in a long time." So, loving a challenge, I called that company first, had the interview with two older gentlemen in suits and - to my extreme delight - got a call from the agency the very next day. I got the job; my first real, full-time job.

Many desks were crammed into that open office space, with partitioned-off cubicles for the managers. Women and men were busy working at data entry (a new field then), bookkeeping, accounts payable, accounts receivables, and purchasing. The sounds of manual typewriters, comptometers, hand-cranked adding machines, people chatting, and phones ringing filled the room non-stop throughout the day. It was so very exciting for me to become a part of the world of business and meet lots of well-educated people with a wide range of skills and interests,

Directly off the elevators was a massive, grey, metal structure. Stenciled in silver on the side were the words IBM MAINFRAME MODEL 705. The front covers to this metal box that we now call a mainframe computer had been removed, exposing its innards. In view for all to see were hundreds of tiny, flickering, colored lights and thousands of thin, color-coded wires, some twisted together in groups as they snaked their way from one part of this strange looking machine to another. Several twelve-inch tape discs rotated at different speeds, changing direction abruptly every few seconds. It was surreal, like something out of a science fiction movie or comic book.

This was the company's first computer and a team of IBM technicians - nerds in blue Oxford shirts with white pocket protectors and thin blue ties - were deep in thought, examining a large electrical schematic diagram taped to the wall. When I left each night at five, they were still hard at work - bleary eyed, ties loosened - engrossed, non-stop checking manuals, notes, moving wires here and there in the machine, and poring over large accordion-folded sheets of paper with rows of small holes running down both edges, filled with strange codes and symbols.

Several young women were learning the art of data entry and each day they produced thousands of data entry cards. Their machines had an electronic keyboard and, with each light tap, quickly punched a small rectangular hole (called a chad) into the rigid three-by-six inch card. This process created a new sound in the modern office that was much like a room-full of upholsterers simultaneously hammering tack after tack into wood. Once the data card was completed, now containing dozens of randomly placed rectangular little holes, the operator pushed a red button and the card was sent at blurring speed over a track into a machine that neatly stacked them twelve inches high. The cards were then automatically fed quickly - one by one – into another machine attached by wires to the computer in the hallway.

This was the beginning of the incomprehensible, fascinating world of computers. Today, that ten-foot wide and six-foot-high computer - which cost millions in 1960s dollars - could be replaced with one small powerful server costing fewer than five thousand dollars, quietly working at speeds a hundred times faster than that first IBM dinosaur.

But this story is not about computers. It's about people at work, their ethical values and behavior, and my memorable, first 'blueprinting' experiences and lessons learned in the world of business. It's about the way my experiences molded my core values as an employee and, later, as an employer.

I entered the business world innocent and naïve, believing that working people are basically good and sincere people who show up to do an honest day's work. It didn't take long for reality to punch me in my ethical face. I learned quickly that I needed to watch my back and be wary of deceitful, divisive, incompetent, lazy and apathetic people. There were also hard-working, decent people blended in with the divisive and lazy.

I quickly discovered that getting ahead often meant climbing over the bodies of co-workers to attain a promotion and more money. Lying, half-truths, exaggeration, and kissing up to the boss often worked to garner a promotion and raise. It was the way 'the game' was played.

I didn't like that game.

I felt then that if I was to be in the business world, I could not take that route to success. I needed to be enthusiastic and competent, and let my boss and fellow workers see that I could be relied upon *one hundred percent* to always do an exceptional job. That work and life ethic was something I acquired from my parents, who prided themselves in being the best at their respective jobs.

One day, after a few weeks on the job, Jay - a young man with freckles and curly red hair - asked me to do something for him in the office. I assumed I was doing something that my boss wanted, so I did what he asked without hesitation. Later that day, my boss, Mr. Ring asked me, "Why did you do that?" I told him that Jay had asked me to do it.

Mr. Ring questioned Jay in my presence, asking him why he had instructed me to do whatever it was at the time. Jay, with a stone-faced demeanor, adamantly denied having asked me to do anything. I was, for the first time in my short career in the business world, 'the deer in the headlights'.

I'm quite certain my boss figured out that Jay was lying, as there would have been no reason for me to do something without being asked. It was my first wake-up call in the business world and I stayed clear of Jay from that day forward.

Some twenty years later I met up with Jay by chance; he was working as a fabric buyer for a children's clothing manufacturer. He didn't recognize me, but I realized almost immediately that he had not changed his stripes. He proceeded to badmouth his employer, telling me things I suspected to be untrue. A month later, he was gone from that job. Even though Jay had a college degree in finance, his mean-spirited and divisive personality continued to sabotage his life.

Then, there was Bernie: a man in his mid-forties who was always very busy, usually with the phone lodged between his neck and shoulder, screaming at someone while simultaneously doodling on the corners of everything in sight. Stacks of paper were piled in disarray on Bernie's desk, but he seemed to know where everything was when needed. He was rough around the edges, wielding crude and foul language to make his point and get the job done. The top button of his shirt was always open and his tie loosened the moment he arrived at his desk in the morning. He often snapped his fingers and barked orders to those who worked directly for him, but he did get the job done and no one really seemed to mind. Bottom line is that I found Bernie to be one of the genuine good guys; kind-hearted and always ready to dole out sensible advice to young people like me, who were just starting out in the business world.

After a year, Bernie left and took a job at another company. He called me from time to time to see how I was doing on the job and to ask if my wife had given birth yet. He was a real mensch, authentic… a good person. Bernie asked if I needed any diapers because his new employer produced them. About a week after my son was born, a large box arrived at my home containing several dozen diapers. Bernie was a genuine guy and my being young and impressionable, his good nature and sincerity resonated with my developing values. I wanted to be like him; not seriously overweight, sloppy, loud and crude, but kind-hearted, genuine and authentic.

My second Monday on the job turned out to be a nightmare for the company. One of their factories, located in Passaic, New Jersey, had burned to the ground on Sunday evening. Because this was a very serious and unfortunate event, everyone in management was focused on trying to figure out what to do. All the raw materials and curtains destroyed by fire, smoke and water had to be replaced immediately, to keep commitments to customers.

The production was shifted to another company factory a hundred and fifty miles away in Massachusetts, but that factory made different kinds of curtains and was not equipped or skilled to produce the needed merchandise. The logistics of ordering machinery, hiring additional manpower, building know-how, and ordering raw materials seemed monumental to me at that time. The alternate factory would need to recruit and train temporary workers immediately, and put on a second and third shift to work seven days a week for a month or longer..

This was a 'blueprinting moment' for me, because I realized that what appeared to be absolutely impossible - when put into the hands of highly skilled, highly motivated, competent and caring employees could and would be done. There have been many times over the years that I've needed to shift into this 'do the impossible' mode in my own business, and my youthful experiences have served me well.

Mr. Ring, a true workaholic and long-time company man, was very much up to the challenge to perform his part in this disastrous event. He was in his glory during the crisis and I learned then how to multi-task and never take your eye off the ball. One whose mantra was 'we can and we *will* do it", Mr. Ring always got the job done and this lesson has served me well over the last fifty years. He worked tirelessly for weeks to *get things back to normal*, arriving early each morning when it was still dark and working long into the night - Saturdays and Sundays included.

Mr. Ring always scribbled on a yellow legal pad, documenting everything anyone said in his presence and on the phone. There were always lots of these pads stacked neatly on his desk, in chronological order. It was his email filing system long before email was invented and he could easily access prior details on any conversation.

Then there was my friend and co-worker, Julius. He and I hit it off at once. He was from the West Indies, an Oxford graduate who worked as a bookkeeper in the accounting department. Julius had a wonderful smile that showed off his three gold teeth, of which he was extremely proud. Julius was the meekest and kindest, best-dressed 'skinny man' I'd ever known. Years later, I met his wife and it was no surprise that she was twice his size; you knew at once who wore the pants.

I believe the company was *comfortable* paying Julius, a black man, less than his white counterparts. He accepted his place as a minority immigrant living in America and rarely complained. I knew then that if I ever had my own business, I'd make sure that the color of a person's skin would not determine their pay scale.

Most paydays, Julius and I would not bring a bag lunch to work, but would go to the chicken rotisserie across from the office and sit at the greasy counter, where we would get a large portion of delicious chicken and fries – with a soda - for under two bucks. Sometimes, when the weather was nice, we would walk to 28th Street, to a charming and affordable restaurant called 'The Library'. We both had financial challenges and I think that enjoying a lunch that neither of us could afford was good for our heads and left us with fond memories of our wonderful friendship. We laughed a lot at lunch, as it was our practice to make fun of our bosses and co-workers.

Carl, Mr. Ring's assistant, was a very friendly man, but a bit of a scatterbrain who spent much of his day animatedly moving papers and folders around his desk and in and out of the drawers. It was amusing to watch his silly 'paper ballet', as he fastidiously choreographed his desk again and again throughout the day. Carl was hard of hearing and struggled with answering the phone. After some time, I took over that task.

Carl was petrified of the executives, especially the Company President, Mr. Bixer, who was admittedly an intimidating character. Bixer's office was tucked away behind the showroom on the main floor. The walls of his office were filled with pictures of him and his family posing in the winner's circle, along with his race horses and jockeys. He was a big man with a deep, raspy voice, who usually sat leaning back in a massive wood and leather chair with a lit Havana clenched in his teeth, smoke billowing above him and lingering near the fluorescent lights.

Mr. Ring usually presented the newest fabrics to Mr. Bixer, the other executives, and the buyers from J.C. Penney, Kresge (now Kmart), and Sears. If Mr. Ring was not in the building and the Big Boss called to see the new fabrics, it was Carl's job to present them. But Carl always got cold feet and would say, "Ted, I'm very busy now, why don't you take these down to Mr. Bixer." After working with Carl a few months, he didn't bother telling me he was busy, just "Please take these down to Bixer." I loved it!

I always jumped at the opportunity to go to the President's office, because I liked the experience of rubbing shoulders with the 'big boys'. Frankly, early on, I adopted the philosophy that 'every man puts his pants on the same way' and, sometimes, to further keep my composure, I pictured the suits tripping all over themselves as they slipped into their shorts.

I had self-confidence and felt that I impressed the President, the buyers and our sales executives with my knowledge of the products and ability to answer all of their questions without hesitation. The more I did this, the more I would notice that Mr. Bixer would speak to me as an equal rather than a lowly gofer. I knew then that, someday, beyond a doubt, I would be one of those well-dressed men earning the big bucks - $20,000 or more. Big money in 1960.

In September of 1960, my first son was born. It was now even more of a financial struggle to come home to a wife and child with a mere $37.50 a week after taxes. My parents and grandparents helped where they could and my wonderful grandmother would, every week or two, spend an hour and a half on three buses to come to my apartment, walk with my wife to the supermarket, and help us to stock up on what we needed.

In 1961, Mr. Ring, Carl and I moved from the open general office on the second floor to a smaller, quieter office on the third. Some very interesting characters visited us each day - mostly salesmen. One young man, Harvey - about thirty - suffered from Tourette syndrome and was what was called a textile broker. He worked for a large firm that bought, sold, and speculated on commodity futures like cotton and synthetic fibers and fabrics.

Harvey always dressed spiffily, had a wife and two young children, and lived out on Long Island. I found him to be an amazing and inspiring human being. He struggled with every word and every uncontrollable twitch, sometimes relapsing into incoherency and sometimes - beyond his control - fits of foul language. I was impressed and inspired by his determination to get past his disability.

Frank, another salesman in his mid-thirties, worked for a large fabric dyeing facility. I thought he was a bit aloof because he totally ignored me. It was because of this that I didn't like him at first, but then, one day, he told me he wanted to give me a free subscription to a textile journal. When asked why, he said he had a good friend who made his living selling subscriptions of the textile journal and who was dying from cancer, but too proud to take money from his friends. To help Frank out, some of his friends were selling subscriptions to their textile industry customers and each man paid for them out of their own pocket. They wanted to make sure their dying friend had an income to support his family while maintaining his dignity. I realized that Frank was a good man and learned then to never judge a book by its cover.

Then there was Marsha, an attractive woman of twenty-five who had been working at the company for almost a year. She had a beautiful figure, long jet-black hair, wore far too much makeup, especially her blackish-red lipstick. She was a comptometer operator, the predecessor to the modern electronic calculator. She was single, wore tight skirts, tighter tops and looked like a Sixties sweater girl. She wore high heels, showing off beautiful muscular calves that could not be ignored. She was pleasant and friendly to everyone, had a good sense of humor, was easy to work with and didn't have 'airs' at the water cooler, as some women did at the time. Her big secret was she was a recovering alcoholic and most nights when she left work, she headed to an AA meeting.

Sitting just a few desks away from her was Rolland. He was a man of forty-one with a wide Hemingway sort of face, ruddy complexion and athletic build. He looked like an artist with a greying beard and full head of salt and pepper hair parted in the center, combed left and right. He was the senior bookkeeper, married with two teenage daughters, and had worked for the company for ten years.

During my first year, Julius and I worked in close proximity to Marsha and Rolland. We observed that they often returned from lunch at exactly the same time, appearing a bit lethargic and disoriented. After a while, we couldn't help noticing the smell of alcohol.

Rolland started to call in sick more and more frequently, as did Marsha - often on the same days. It became clear to everyone in the office that *something* was going on between them. At first, we thought they may be having an affair, which could also have been true. At some point, we found out that Rolland was also a recovering alcoholic and it appeared that his marriage was now falling apart, so he was again hitting the bottle.

Rolland and Marsha were making lots of accounting mistakes and one Friday afternoon they were each asked to report separately to the personnel department on the third floor. They were promptly fired for drinking on the job and excessive absences.

When they returned to the second floor, each let everyone know that they had been fired. It was a very sad Friday for all of us because we genuinely liked both of them and also understood how devastating and embarrassing this must be for them. We all agreed that they needed to get a handle on their drinking problem or there would be more days like this in their futures.

Marsha, teary-eyed, with mascara running down her face, came over to me, gave me a hug, and wished me well with the new baby and good luck with my future. She told me she thought I would go far.

Then Rolland returned to the office and quietly said goodbye to each person, his head hanging down in shame and embarrassment. He picked through his desk for his personal belongings, face white as a ghost. He looked up one last time, waved to everyone and walked out on a ten-year job. There were no warnings and second chances back then. After a week, there were new people at the desks.

I often wondered what happened to Marsha and Rolland. Did they get help and put their lives back on a sober track? Were they romantically involved? Did they marry or did they end up living lives dictated by alcohol?

Over the years, I learned a lot from the people I worked with and worked for, including the value of hard work, attention to detail, treating everyone with respect, being honest - and much, much more. I'd like to believe that I took those life lessons seriously and to heart and that I've been a good role model for the people who work and have worked for me, for my suppliers and customers, and most important, for my kids.

MOURNING MORNING

Today, morning arrived and I did not wake.

The birds tried to wake me, as they often did. The children playing in the street below tried to wake me with their shrill screams and laughter, but I did not stir. Impatient motorists honking and motorcyclists revving their engines, anticipating the green light, also tried in vain.

The mailman often greets the hard-of-hearing Miss Ruff with a loud and whimsical onomatopoeic "Good morning, Miss Rrruff!" but this does not wake me today - nor does anything else breathing life into this new day on earth.

Why, I ask myself, why? And I suddenly realize why. I passed in my sleep. I did not know when I brushed my teeth, closed my book and turned off the light last night, that I would never brush my teeth again, never look in the mirror again, never kiss my children and grandchildren or any other living soul again.

The list of 'to do tomorrow' scribbled in my shorthand and lying on the kitchen table, waiting for me to look it over with my coffee today, will become part of my final legacy for my children to save or cast away.

Meet Harry t'day for lun 12:15 at the caf. Pay elec and pho, call Peg, rice, tomat, lamb, cat fd.

Missy rubs the right front leg of the kitchen table, turns and returns to rub her other side. She purrs, jumps on the chair, surveys the table, then jumps up on it - as she's done for years – and stares at the untouched list as if she could read it. My cat contemplates her empty bowl, now crusty from dinner. She meows several times into the bowl, hoping this will make some food appear.

She and I are both mourning morning today, and now we wait to be found.

MILLIONS OF TREES WILL BE SAVED!

We are news, photos, graphics - all printed on cellulose, mostly from tree pulp. Each morning, we provide global and local news, sports and weather. We attract those with a passion for electronics and celebrity trash, dream cars and sailboats. We entertain lovers of rock climbing and rock music, inform the bucket list generation where to go and what to do next. We reveal the latest fad diet and predict next season's fashion.

Like bread, we are prepared while people sleep and, like milk in the past, delivered to their door before breakfast. We are read with morning coffee, on the chaise, at the beach, in the hotel lobby, and on the bus, plane, and train.

We are journals for music lovers, academics, business folk, politicians, doctors, men and women of the cloth, and board game lovers. We promise adventure, knowledge, enjoyment, wealth, and the latest strategies to win at bridge. We start as a small pile of unread periodicals and Sunday newspapers, and soon we stand a foot high. We are pounds of slick pictures and fascinating articles, just waiting for your attention.

The mounting pile becomes an eyesore and our readers barely notice. Since there is a long weekend or trip planned, they say they will read us later, but rarely do. The frequent traveler whispers, *"I'll read you all on my trip and come back light as a feather."* The destination is reached and most of us are still waiting to hear our spines cracked or have our pages flipped.

They fall asleep with us at their side, still unread, while loosely holding the remote. Some of us actually return home, still unread, and are piled on a shelf near the stairs or in the kitchen with used plastic and paper bags.

Weeks pass. We've become invisible. There are ball games, PTA meetings, birthdays, dinner dates, the beach, a barbecue, Thanksgiving dinner, trick-or-treaters at the door, and building a snowman before the weather gets too warm. We wait while our news and information becomes less relevant with each passing day - week - month. Some of us now share space with current news and the latest journals, and the predictions we made now seem foolish, irrelevant and - far too often - embarrassingly wrong.

The phone rings. Out-of-town friends are unexpectedly close by and spontaneously are invited or invite themselves over for cocktails. They must declutter at once! We are hastily gathered up and plopped onto the cold basement floor.

Some of us have traveled from coast to coast and back, have been jammed between supermarket weekend newspaper inserts and lowly coupons, thumbed, skimmed and still not read. Some of us are used to wrap garbage, clean windows, start the fire.

Not long ago, we represented the news of the day, superseding everything that arrived a day, week or month before. Our magazine articles were interesting, inspiring and the cutting edge on every subject known to mankind.

We hear the 'beep - beep - beep' of the garbage truck backing up into the incinerator bay and it's our time to become smoke and ash. Page by printed page, we smolder and say goodbye to humanity.

Someday we may never be printed at all. Our messages, our pictures, our information will be viewed on demand on a screen at home or in your hand. There will be no need for humans to feel guilty at the print piling high and not being read, because millions of trees will be saved.

That is of course, if there are any trees.

FISH TALE

Sitting on a stool at the sushi bar, one could peer through the beads of condensation on the refrigerated display case and see the standard chunks of lush salmon, dark red tuna, dense yellowtail, colorful octopus, and other assorted sea creatures.

In a flash, a moment of surreal disbelief, each shapeless piece of fish comes to life and returns to its whole fish DNA. The display is suddenly filled with crystal-clear water and now hungry fish are swimming inside from one end to the other looking for food.

The fish can see their human meal outside the display case. It's the sushi chef on one side, still slicing up their friends and, on the other, patrons busy stuffing their faces with sushi rolls and sashimi. A sushi chef does not notice the changes in the display case and, as he's done thousands of times before, slides open the display door to retrieve a large chunk of yellowtail. He's struck by excruciating pain as the yellowtail bites off his forefinger up to the knuckle.

As he screams in pain and withdraws his hemorrhaging hand, an octopus tentacle grabs him by the wrist and attempts to yank him into the display case. Water rushes out of the case. He pulls away with the help of a coworker and lands on the large wood sticky rice dispenser.

There is pandemonium at the sushi bar and in the restaurant. On one side, patrons jump up and knock over tables behind them, occupied by patrons with elaborate sushi platters. The prepared delicacies - now also in fish form - flap around until they fall off the table, filling the floor of the restaurant with live fish banging about in pursuit of water.

The three sushi chefs are screaming in Japanese, and the Thai waitress and Jewish owner rush over to see what has caused such a commotion, each slipping on the fish, some losing their balance and falling, to be bitten by the larger fish and dragged around by octopus tentacles.

In a flash, *things return to normal.*

The sushi chefs will forevermore fear for their fingers each time they slide the display case door open and reach for a chunk of fish. Many of the patrons who witnessed this will never enter a sushi restaurant again; others will consider that their sushi or sashimi could at any moment become the fish it once was - and if it came from a big fish, like tuna, could even take a chunk out of their hand.

Some go on to relate the strange happenings to others, but no one had their cell phone handy to record the incident so they aren't believed. However, it was a remarkable and memorable moment for those who did witness this fish tale.

BUZZ AT THE RED LION INN

The afternoon sun drifts through the sheer white curtains onto the dining room tables. Each table is adorned in white linen, cream-colored china, silver place settings, and exquisite autumn flower arrangements surrounded with yellow crookneck squash, multicolor gourds, and tiny pumpkins.

The traditional Thanksgiving dinner crowd is now ensconced in the large dining room at the Red Lion Inn. The polite and subdued buzz is broken only by small children's need to be heard. It's a symphony of family sounds and a classic scene right off the tip of Norman Rockwell's charcoal pencil. The children's outbursts accentuate the mood and give it color and credibility, unwittingly reminding us that the future really is theirs.

Here we have three generations revisiting the long-observed tradition of Thanksgiving dinner at the Red Lion Inn, started by past generations long gone but present today - in spirit - with the living for one more year. Even though the internet has kept most in touch, there is nothing like a real tight hug, a kiss, face-to-face, eye-to-eye conversations, sharing libations, memories, and dreams. The most senior, often letting their guard down after their second glass of wine, reveal family secrets that under sober circumstances would remain untold.

The little girl in the high chair last year is now proudly sitting on a pillow on her own grown-up chair, her golden pigtails swinging with every awkward move. The teen boy remains quiet and self-conscious about his acne, not knowing if the girls at the next table are giggling at him and, if so, why?

Together once again, they romance the past, celebrate kids starting kindergarten or going off to college, and nostalgically remember family members and friends that have passed on this year. Grandparents have planned to take this festive occasion to announce that they will be picking up John's first year of college or helping with the down payment on a new home. There is joy at this table today. There is joy in the air and all around.

The plump waitress - hiding much of her corpulence behind her loose black dress and white apron - rushes with her tray from tables to kitchen, kitchen to bar, bar to tables, doing her very best to keep everyone happy (and hopefully maximizing those crucial tips that help pay the rent and the grocery bills).

The latest adult generation orchestrates the American dream, toasts to their successes and the year ahead, imbibes and brushes off their disappointments as life's challenges. Oblivious to the small talk, the children sit content, their electronic games making life far easier for everyone here than for the last generation.

Moment by precious moment, Thanksgiving keeps on giving. It brings out the best in us as families reunite to celebrate and to grow together spiritually. Frame by freeze-frame, they recall events of the past, laugh together and feel good to be reunited.

The Red Lion Inn. One of the thousands of inns and restaurants across our continent where *everyone* celebrates, regardless of their ethnic, religious or political preference; where we all come together today and give thanks for the incredible luck of the draw... to be born in America.

BEYOND THE FACE

It's quiet. Thursday morning at the local coffee shop and I'm alone except for a bald, crouched-over old man at the very last table, wearing a beautiful bright-blue cable-knit sweater. I could almost hear him sucking the information from the local newspaper into his head.

'Bye, Bye, Miss American Pie' is playing over and over. It's soothing and allows me to concentrate. A cute young blond is noisily moving fresh pastries off a baking tray onto aluminum foil in the display cases. Another waitress is topping off the salt and sugar dispensers, replenishing the napkins, and wiping down the table tops. I get a whiff of the ammonia and think, "Is she out to lunch or just inconsiderate?" as the acrid smell overwhelms the sweet aroma of my blueberry cupcake and fresh coffee.

I've come here this morning to plan the next few months: trips to a Las Vegas trade show, to London and Brussels, and to Athens, Greece to visit my daughter, with plans for us to go together to Paris to celebrate my seventy-fifth birthday.

I look back at the old man. He's nodded off and his head is bobbing back and forth. I'm wondering if he has plans for the rest of the day, the week, the month, and will there be another year of life for him? I don't know him, but at the moment - for some stupid and arrogant reason - I feel I have the right to judge him as just another lonely old man passing one day at a time. I feel sorry for his boring life, both past and present.

A week later, I return to the coffee shop and the old man is sitting at a table with some friends of mine. He is now very animated and discussing his trip to Europe. I find out that he's a very famous concert pianist who still travels around the world and is in great demand by all the major symphony halls.

So now, when I see someone who looks like he or she may have a boring life, I think twice. I have found that - even though many people do have uneventful existences - many have amazing skills as writers, singers, musicians, artists, dancers, chemists, brain surgeons, acrobats, jugglers, animal trainers, politicians, actors, jet fighters and commercial airline pilots, as well as famous athletes in the fields of tennis, golf, baseball, football, soccer, hockey – even a gold medal holder and someone who in his youth conquered Mount Everest.

So now, instead of looking down on strangers, I fantasize and give each that I see a unique skill or occupation. "That old woman sitting alone at the train station; what was her life about?" I think. Perhaps she is a professor of physics and has, in her lifetime, developed amazing concepts and hypotheses that are revealed in her many books – some used by the most advanced physics courses and translated into many languages. Somewhere along her life's track, she got married, gave birth to four children and now has twelve grandchildren. She is waiting for the train to take her to Boston, where she will meet her family, who have flown in from around the country to celebrate her receiving a lifetime achievement award from Harvard University's President - the university she retired from ten years ago as a full professor.

Or she may be on her way to Philadelphia to visit her dying mother of ninety-five, a Holocaust survivor. Or she could be visiting her twin sister with whom she performed at Radio City Music Hall as a Rockette, both later having supporting roles in a host of popular movies.

Think of an old, retired pilot flying cross country as a passenger to see his grandchildren. Somehow the pilot and co-pilot get food poisoning and are out cold, and there is no one to take the controls and land the plane. A stewardess asks over the public address system if there is a commercial pilot on the plane. The old man raises his hand and, as he moves slowly through the aisle with the aid of a cane, everyone questions the old man's ability, thinking, "He doesn't look like a pilot."

They no longer question his age or his skill when he has safely landed the plane and saved all of their lives.

BEEP, BEEP!

The dusty, old, rusted and badly dented dark-green Chevy twists and maneuvers through the slow-moving morning traffic. Juan, the nervous father-to-be, his hand pressed relentlessly on the horn, is attempting to deliver his pregnant wife to the hospital, though the prospect of delivering the child in the car is becoming a very real possibility.

Maria struggles, leans left and right, anticipating the car's sudden lane changes, acceleration, and shortstops. Her water has already broken and she's sitting uncomfortably in the wetness. Periodically, she arches her waist to relieve the mounting pain and cramps as her contractions grow closer together and longer.

Juan, sweat dripping down his spine and beading his forehead, struggles to make headway, but his horn is ignored or not heard through the closed windows of the drivers around him. If only his horn could scream: "My wife is having a baby, please let me through!" If only.

In the back seat, Juan and Maria's mothers - stiff-lipped with worry - stoically gaze out the windows, converse softly in Spanish and, with begging glances and hand gestures out the windows, try to persuade drivers to the left and right to yield to their horn's pleas.

Motorists always yield to flashing lights and police, fire-engine and ambulance sirens seen in their rear-view mirrors, but they show indifference and disdain for the run-of-the-mill horn-honker with an unknown agenda. They spitefully ignore the horn and hold their ground.

The next time you hear a frantic horn, give the driver the benefit of the doubt and let them pass, because there may just be a new life on the way. Consider that, long ago, it may have been *your* mother and father rushing you to be born.

PASSING TORCHES

Young people seventeen to nineteen gather outside a Starbucks in an upscale suburb of Athens, Greece. So they can smoke, they sit at a table outside. The boys are in baggy jeans and talking tees with their sleeves rolled up to show muscle. The girls arrive in cut-down, fashionably ragged denim shorts with the pocket lining dangling, and tight tops exposing enough skin to make their fathers blush. All are enjoying a lazy Sunday afternoon together, as each competes for attention with loud, disruptive laughter, wild hand and face gestures, and foul language. They push the envelope in their roles as the obnoxiously immature, knowing full well that they are upsetting others around them, and they consider it very cool.

Making dramatic contorted lip and mouth shapes, they blow smoke rings up inside the large umbrella. The boys talk about music, soccer, motorcycles, their latest video games; they dream out loud of the car and speedboat of their dreams, and - in hushed tones - about their latest conquest, usually more fantasy than fact. The young women are all about makeup, cosmetics, the newest nail colors, celebrity trash, and a good-looking teacher. The girls always break their promises and tell what they've sworn to keep secret, like who's sleeping with whom this week.

Despina - a petite, homely blond, tattoo sleeve up her left arm and a gold nostril ring - slips uninvited onto Stathi's lap, a cute guy with his hoodie up lookin' cool. Despina, not yet in touch with her dignity, kisses him raveningly on his neck and face as he pulls away. His machismo ignores her fingers reaching down the back of his shirt. Stathi puffs away on his Marlboro Lights, laughing attentively at the comments of some of the others, registering the sexually charged body language coming from Roula, an attractive and busty blond diagonally across the table.

After an hour, they're all antsy to move on, and when the first person gets up, they all follow, blow kisses in the air, exchange superficial hugs, and quickly depart. They leave behind a pile of paper cups, butt-filled ashtrays, two crumpled cigarette boxes, and many empty packets of sugar.

The table is cleaned and minutes later a group of fashionably dressed men and women in their early thirties arrive. The screeching of chairs commences as they are collected from other tables, preparing for the arrival of others that will join them. Two sets of parents arrive with state-of-the-art jogging strollers; each locked and loaded with fashionably dressed little boys of three. When settled, the toddlers twist their heads from side to side, watching each other and catching the hand waves and facial expressions of the group. The men laugh and exchange new jokes about the prime minister, their work experiences from the week past, soccer, the government in general, their next or last vacation, the government again, and the latest promotions at work. They curse the new taxes, impending strikes, hype a new restaurant, and of course, the battle of the bulge.

The women discuss the children's diets, the pre-schools they want them to attend next year, their lack of satisfaction with the domestic help, a new recipe, the latest fashion, some gossip about their mutual friends getting engaged or divorced, and of course... the battle of the bulge.

After an hour, Alexis gets a call and, after engaging in conversation for a few minutes, tells the group that he needs to leave to deal with a problem with the contractor building his new summer home. Moments later everyone else gets up to move on. The men reach out with a one-arm 'man hug' to the other men and a pair of cheek kisses in the wind to the women. The women give each other a full body hug and kisses, and promise each other to meet again soon; they all go their separate ways.

This group has made it out of their twenties and has settled confidently and comfortably into their thirties. Most have prospered, some have stopped smoking - at least near the children - have swapped the sweet coffee drinks for black coffee or tea, and have given up the rich cakes for fruit and yogurt. They appear comfortable and confident in their mature skins and in their roles as responsible adults, parents, and breadwinners.

For this group, youthful experimentation, rowdy behavior and 'pushing the envelope' has passed, no more than a blurred memory to share in old age with their contemporaries. They have advanced on the grand board game of life to adulthood, as they prepare the way for their children, still in strollers, to grow into the next generation of teens who will unwittingly mimic their parent's youthful behavior and experimentation, pushing the envelope, looking for adolescent acceptance in all the wrong places and in all the wrong ways. This will be their window in time for immature behavior, as they get together to smoke, flirt and experiment with sex, eat sweets, drink strong coffee, flirt more, curse, and show off their youthfully tight and beautiful bodies to the world... and flirt a little more.

The responsible adults have passed the torch. One day, in the hard-to-imagine future, their children will dance intoxicated, with a cell phone in hand, on the top of a bar until the sun rises over the Aegean.

TIME GOD

Glancing into and transfixed by the mirror,
the second hand dances counter-clockwise behind me,
laughing at the time god.

On the treadmill of life,
we tick off daily tasks,
rushing indiscriminately from one chore to another.

For the ambitious,
time is the elusive bird
racing across the sky from dawn to dusk,
from sunrise to moonrise.

For the lazy and indifferent, time is happily masticating,
plotting the avoidance of work, remaining on the couch,
getting others to do the work and take out the dog,
always conniving cash-for-beer without work.

For the downtrodden, hungry, incarcerated, enslaved,
time is a dismal never-ending day-by-day numbing-down,
becoming the norm of daily existence,
unfathomable for those of us never trapped in that world.

For the negative, bitter, angry, evil, jealous and
    mean-spirited,
loss and pain is always someone else's fault,
someone else's problem... both.

For the ignorant,
time is but a word
without meaning or reference,
to be compared with nothing.

For the very old and terminally ill,
time is quickly running out,
anticipating the next or last meal,
hoping for the relief that sleep and unconsciousness
    provide,
wishing for a quiet passing
to a pain-free place.

Life. Regardless of how many moments are present at the
    beginning or end,
it's in all those before birth and after death,
that we are totally and truly alone.
After all, death is a private matter.

With every tick of time,
with each revolution of the earth,
with every breath,
with each heartbeat,
we grow more aware of our soul and our decline.

So, birth and death... it's life's answer to *every little thing*.

PASSION HUT

Bare and tender city feet sink into the sand along a peaceful stretch of beach on a quiet little island in the Caribbean. The sound of highly therapeutic and euphoric waves crashing onto the beach races towards them. Some say the sound of the waves is the best natural aphrodisiac.

They mingle sweaty palms, perspiration dripping from forehead to brow, eyes squinting at the sun's thousand glittering reflections on the blue-green sea. They breathe in the bobbing white-heads of surf and the fresh salty air.

They stop for a moment to kiss and their hearts now beat faster and faster, passions rising. They say in unison, "I love you." They say it again and again, and laugh between themselves, happy to be together and alone. Now, their legs move them in lock step back to the straw-and-bamboo hut on the beach - with a single purpose.

They enter the hut and don't seem to mind the hornets buzzing busily above them. In this quiet moment, she reaches back and pulls the strings of her bikini top. It falls to the ground and her velvet skin - sparkling from the white mica sand, begging to be touched - represents everything that makes them alive and *in the moment*.

She lies down on the thin mat, reaches up, and with her hands on his neck, pulls him on top of her. An erotic buzz is loud inside them; it blocks the surf, the seagulls and even the ominous hornets in the peak of their hut.

At this moment, the planet could be on fire and they would not notice or even care. It's the moment every living human seeks unconsciously; the moment directed by their caveman (and woman) DNA: to make love, procreate and keep their species alive.

Believe in God or not, something greater than us alone is at work here.

May the force be with you today.

SUCKERS FOR THE
SNOW-COVERED BEGGAR

Dear Sis and Brother,

You will be reading this after I have passed on and, hopefully, because you are both younger, you will still be enjoying your lives. I've left my inheritance to the two of you and, should either or both of you pass on, the inheritance will go equally to your wonderful children... who were also the children Max and I never had.

Unknown to you and everyone but Max, I've had a rather 'unusual' secret life that I would now like to share with the two of you. As weird, incredible, and unbelievable as it may sound, this is one hundred percent true and Max, if he were still alive when you read this, would attest to it. Except for a few people high up in our government, no one else knows what I am about to tell you.

First, I was not the 'bookkeeper' that I always claimed to be for those thirty years before Max and I retired. I tried bookkeeping for a while, but hated the work and being cooped up in an office all day. However, like many working women, I woke early, prepared breakfast and sandwiches for lunch for Max and myself, and went into the streets. My job kept me on the street all day, regardless of the weather and, no, I was not a hooker.

For thirty years, when I got dressed for work, I transformed myself into a street beggar. My goal was to attract kind-hearted souls and suckers with spare change. When I first proposed this strange 'career move' to Max, he thought I'd lost my mind, but then - when he pondered the tax advantage from his accountant's point of view and envisioned all the nice tax-free cash - he realized it was a brilliant idea and we became cohorts. Actually, he confessed after the first year that part of him did not seriously expect the begging thing to last long-term - perhaps only until it got too hot or too cold on the street, or I got bored with the work or lack of it. That never happened. I loved being on the street, free from the restrictions and drudgery of a normal job, and the office politics which I disliked.

On one occasion, Carmen, one of my neighbors, came by when I was on the street and gave me some change, looked at me in a puzzled way, but said nothing. Then, when I saw her at the elevator one day, she said, "You know, you have a double. It's a poor woman on the street. I always give her whatever change I have when I see her." I bit my lip because I would have liked to say, "The most you ever gave me was a dime and a few pennies – cheapie!"

On other occasions through the years, I did see people I knew, but they were always preoccupied, usually looking down into their phone screens, always rushing off somewhere; none ever gave me a focused glance.

Being on the street in one spot all day gave me a perspective much different than being a pedestrian rushing by. I would see and hear everything going on around me in magnified, crystal-clear, high-resolution detail. I liked to see myself as an iguana on an uninhabited south sea island, perched on a rock, and basking in the sun right off the beach. (The thought developed from a short story I read years ago by a famous Russian author.) The iguana blended into the flora and, while not moving for hours, experienced every slight breeze on its face, and heard the barely audible sounds of rustling grass and the booming waves crashing on the sandy beach. Like the iguana, which could hear the high-pitched sound of an approaching bug fifty feet away and, at just the right moment, uncoil its long tongue for the catch, I - in the same fashion - could sense a sucker or kind soul approaching. I'd hold out my cup at just the right moment and, with a sad, pathetic, hungry look on my face, gaze up to manifest my misery and wishful anticipation of a small handout, a pittance for 'this poor and unfortunate street lady'.

In summer, I would wear a light raincoat and, in winter, a fur-lined trench coat. I would take my small, battered and dirty suitcase and cover it with a custom-made, clean burlap cover so that only the handle protruded, lest a neighbor or someone I knew and met in the street recognized the suitcase as the beggar's. Once I reached my begging spot for the day, I'd look around to make sure no one saw me as I removed the burlap cover and placed it inside the suitcase.

I kept the suitcase mostly empty because I took the subway from time to time and could then easily carry it up and down the stairs. In the winter, the suitcase contained a lightweight, high-quality goose down quilt, covered with a waterproof liner. I would throw an old stained blanket on top of it, sit down and wrap one end of the blanket around me. I placed a thick, insulated foam cushion under my butt for comfort and protection from the cold, winter sidewalk.

A rain-free Friday was usually the best day to beg because most people are more generous after they've cashed their paycheck. Even if they have direct deposit, they often did lunch on payday with coworkers, so they'd have cash in their pockets and liked to impress each other with their generosity and kindness. I stayed near the restaurants each Friday; the ones where I knew people to be the best givers and suckers. It was not the expensive restaurants that worked well, because there the big shots were too busy impressing their clients on the way in and out, and they just didn't look down. Sometimes these well-dressed men and women just jumped in and out of a limo, so they were of no value to a street beggar. It was mostly the middle class and lower class that easily parted with their spare change and the way many of them dressed, they could be living hand-to-mouth, but they were also very generous. I think they identified with the plight of the underdog and homeless and were appreciative to have a job and a roof over their heads.

I admit, I did at times feel *momentary* guilt taking money from those that had little to share, but - hey - if they didn't give it to me, they would give it to someone else for drugs or cheap wine, or spend it on themselves for an unhealthy sugary snack. So, I was actually doing them a favor. I couldn't actually say to them: "Keep it; you probably need it more than me." It was at those times, I would think of the million dollars plus – tax-free cash! - that I'd squirreled away over the years in several safe deposit boxes.

Rain on Fridays was a bummer. One would think that people would be more charitable and sympathetic to a poor, old woman sitting on the street in the rain, but they were usually carrying an open umbrella in one hand, and a bag or briefcase in the other, so not getting wet was generally their priority over considering me, a poor drenched beggar. The really good people stopped, closed their umbrella, and got wet while searching for some change for me. They were the best suckers!

The very best time to beg was when I was covered in snow. It's highly dramatic and effective, and the snow clearly stimulated many people's 'help-the-needy' gene. And since most people don't use an umbrella in the snow, they had a free hand to reach for change and stretch out their arm to deposit it in my slightly crumpled paper cup. They were my classic 'suckers for the snow-covered beggar'.

There were some regulars who recognized me and always handed me some change as if it was their obligation to help an old friend, or perhaps they just came from church or on their way to confession and wanted to be sure that God thought well of them. You know what I mean? I never missed a Friday in the snow. It was like having a winning scratch ticket.

It's amazing, but in all my years in the harshest of elements, I was only sick once. That day, I came to work on the street with tissues, blowing my red nose all day, and it was my best day…ever! Actually, I think that I avoided sickness because, in addition to eating healthy and taking vitamins, being in the elements each day had given me a very strong immune system. For added protection in inclement weather, I always wore a waterproof shower cap under my hat so my head stayed warm and dry.

Old and lonely women often tried to engage me in conversation, but I avoided speaking, making believe I didn't understand, and just showed my 'thankful' smile. I'd repeat over and over, bending from the waist again and again, "Thank you, please, thank you – thank you." Sometimes, if I saw they were wearing a crucifix, I would say "God bless" and they absolutely loved that. At times, they became emotional, all teary-eyed and often so thankful for what 'they have and I don't', they would come up with more change and sometimes a buck or a fiver. They should only know - ha-ha! I really felt I'd done these people a service because they could feel 'closer to God' and have a greater appreciation for what they had. And I got the cash like I was their psychiatrist or personal coach.

Each day, I ended up with a lot of small change and my thankful burden was to lug the heavy booty home, especially up and down the subway stairs when I couldn't catch a bus. When I got home, I would run the coins through my change sorting machine and load them into paper rolls to change at the bank. Max took the heavy rolls to the bank a few times a week before work. One day, I counted 322 pennies, 42 nickels, 78 dimes and, believe it or not, 89 quarters. And, on top of this, I had 21 crumpled dollar bills and one new five. So, my take that day was $60.92, and that was for a mere four hours in the street on a windy, cold day with snow flurries. By the end of my career, my average take was about $375 a week, tax-free of course. My husband said that it would be like earning almost $550 a week and, since I was not 'officially' on anyone's payroll, he was able to take me as a second dependent. Even though I never collected social security, Max said we were still way ahead of the game.

When I started begging, Max and I decided that we would save all my earnings for retirement. His salary was sufficient for us to live on and his company provided a pension plan and free adequate medical insurance for us both. We dreamed about traveling the world first class, to all those exotic places we always read about.

From time to time, when I got bored, I took the subway down to the financial district, where I often got a buck or a fin from the suits and - in a good week - could make up to six hundred bucks. There was a lot of competition in the Wall Street area, so I had to pick my days and locations carefully to make sure I wouldn't get into hassles with the local street people, who could be violent and try to steal what I made. Many unfortunately supported a drug or drinking habit but some were just certified loonies. I usually picked inclement days, when the local beggars were less likely to venture out of the shelters.

I kept all of my savings in safe deposit boxes in three different banks. Sometimes I would take a day off and go to one of the banks to 'visit my money'. I always added more cash and, if time permitted, would meet a friend for lunch at a nearby fancy restaurant.

With the million-plus tucked away, as well as other savings, Max and I took early retirement. We would continue to help the CIA. (I'll tell you about that later.)

There were mostly legitimate down-and-out people on the street, far more men than women. Many were alcoholics or druggies, and many were mentally disturbed humans, struggling with their limited ability just to survive and get through the day in the best way they could. Yesterday was a blur to them and tomorrow wasn't a concept most of them had the ability to embrace. It was all about the here and now. I always avoided speaking with the other street people. First, I was a beggar by profession and choice and, unlike them, I left the street every evening for my nice home and loving husband. I didn't want to build relationships with any of these people and possibly blow my cover or get emotionally involved with their tragic lives on the street, even though I often wondered how each of them ended up at the bottom of society's barrel in the land of opportunity.

Street people have their own subculture: a network of sharing and trading street secrets, like the location of a warm and safe place to sleep, or where food or cigarettes are being handed out as a promotion, and, of course, any new soup kitchen and shelter on their turf. Some of these people have been on the street for many years and one would think that - knowing how dangerous the winters were on the street - they would try to go south in the late fall, like homeless 'snow birds' seeking a warm place to sleep without fear of freezing to death.

For those that did escape the cold, when they returned in the Spring, they were always sad to find out about those that didn't make it through the winter: those who succumbed to the cold, to drugs, alcohol, lack of medical care, and violence in and out of the shelters. They suffered from poor or nonexistent hygiene - often not bathing for weeks - which created terrible infections and body sores, causing them to constantly scratch and inflame those areas further. Sometimes they huddled together for warmth or safety, and they transferred infections and lice, among other things. Eating out of garbage bins on the street subjected them to rickets, worms, dysentery, and they were often found lifeless when the sun rose the next day. Most had rotting teeth or no teeth at all, so their ability to eat nourishing food was compromised. If they got a tooth or gum infection, it often because so inflamed that they could end up with a heart condition or stroke. Malnutrition was rampant, especially if they had a drug or alcohol addiction; they would eat very little nourishing food and a body can survive just so long living like that.

Many years ago, I was sitting outside a nail salon and, each day, I would see some unsavory looking Asian men bringing young women into a building. I noticed that the women never came out. The women were all Asian and seemed to work long hours in the nail salon. This disturbed me because it looked like they may be indentured laborers or slaves, smuggled into the country and being held against their will. I thought about it long and hard for two weeks and discussed it with Max each night. I wanted to go to the police but was afraid to blow my cover, and local police are sometimes corrupt and on the take, working with these dangerous criminal types. In the end, I decided that I needed to tell the authorities. I decided on the CIA. I went to their downtown office, dressed nicely, and told them about what was happening at the nail salon.

When they asked me how I was able to observe all of this for so long, I told them that I liked to sit in this area, especially on a sunny day. It turned out that I was right and not only were they using these girls as slaves during the day in the salon, but they were also using them as sex slaves at night. The entire ring of about 40 men and women were arrested after a major sting and all the girls, about sixty in total, were set free and returned to their families in the U.S. and Asia.

About six months later, I received a phone call from a lady at the CIA's headquarters. She was one of the CIA's top local brass in the area and asked me if I could stop by and see her. When I arrived at her office she asked me if I would like to work on a special project. I was shocked, to say the least, The CIA wanted me to work for them?

The woman, who will remain nameless, told me that - after I turned in the gang of human smugglers - they followed me to see if I was from a rival gang, trying to put the competition out of business. They saw exactly what my game was and how I was pretending to be a homeless beggar. The woman told me that they needed an undercover person to watch and report on the comings and goings of certain individuals in a midtown building. Because there was no parking or standing on that busy midtown street, they could not plant an undercover van at the scene. She told me that no one would suspect me, a street beggar.

They said they would pay me $75 a day in cash for as long as the surveillance lasted. They gave me a sophisticated video camera built into a small, banged-up, innocent-looking box and it would record the comings-and-goings in the area.

The information was wirelessly transmitted to a receiver close by and then sent to their headquarters, where it was recorded and scrutinized.

This went on for a little over three weeks. At the end of each week, a man would come by and drop an envelope in my lap with the cash promised; always careful to make sure that no one saw him. I never did find out what happened in that case because, when I asked, I was told that they could not say for my own protection. However, I am quite certain that the undercover work was a success because they called on me often and posted me at various places around the city for different investigations. I was a great asset for them because I was not really a street person and could be depended on. They knew I would not blow their cover, and I knew they would not blow mine.

Once, after being posted for a month outside a building in Little Italy, I was told not to show up again, and the very next day the outcome was all over the news. There was a major raid and about thirty men were arrested as part of a protection and gambling racket.

One day, my CIA contact asked me if my husband and I would be interested in going on a Caribbean cruise, all expenses paid. They needed surveillance on a couple that was apparently suspected of espionage. The mission was to plant listening devices in various areas on the ship once we discovered where they would spend their time. The very first evening, we saw the table they were assigned to in the dining room, so we waited until the wait staff had left and planted a device under their table. The couple also enjoyed sitting on the second deck – midship - and we were able to plant another device within earshot, behind one of the donut-shaped life preservers. We had a transmittal box in our room and all we needed to do was plug it in; the device would record everything and send it along to the CIA via satellite.

The ship's food was wonderful and, better still, we were paid $5,000 in addition to the cost of the trip, which was $8,000. We went on many trips like this and saw much of the world, compliments of the U.S. government. Ironically, I had not paid taxes for thirty years and wouldn't have to pay taxes on the money given to us by the CIA. How funny is that?

On one of our cruises, a woman approached me and said, "You look very familiar, do I know you?"

"Yes", I said, slowly, with a big grin. "We have met," but I didn't offer any more information.

After she realized I was not giving her any details, she said with a bit of annoyance, "Where *do* you know me from?"

After a small hesitation, I gathered my bravado and said, "Did you ever use the subway at 86th Street and Broadway in Manhattan?"

She responded quickly "Yes, quite often. But how would you know that?"

I continued, "Did you ever give some small change to a street beggar at the station?"

She then stared at me for an uncomfortable ten seconds and said, "Yes, what does that have to do with anything?"

I realized then that she probably never made eye contact with me, and hadn't looked at anything but my ragged clothing and wrinkled cup - that's quite common on the street.

"What I mean," I said with a big smile, looking her straight in the eye, "is I am that person."

Her eyes and mouth opened wide, her head jerked back - aghast - and she said in a confused state, "But that's not possible. That was a street beggar!"

"Yes," I said, very cheerfully, tilting my head up, as if I

were thumbing my nose at her. "And I would like to *thank you* for all of all the change you put in my cup over the years. You are a very charitable woman."

She backed away without a word and avoided me through the balance of the cruise. On the last day, just before disembarking, she came over to me, looking down and not making eye contact at first. She said quietly, "I am sorry that I judged you as I did. I never thought I would see a woman that was begging in the street on a first-class cruise, even though you have as much right to be here as I do - and perhaps even more, because I've never worked a day in my life and what you were doing was work, in a fashion".

I thanked her and told her that she would not be seeing me on the street anymore because I had retired. Before we departed, I said to her, "My husband and I have no children, so we decided to travel the world in our retirement." I then thanked her for reaching out and for helping street people. Before she walked away, I grabbed her arm and said, "I'm sure that you will not find others like me. Unfortunately, most street beggars are just *that* and they live to survive one day at a time. It really is sad and I do hope that you will continue to help them when you can." She nodded in agreement and walked away.

So, my dear sister and brother, now you know it all. I ask that you not share this information with anyone - first to protect the CIA and, second, so street beggars will not be suspected of being phonies like me. And by-the-way, since most of this money came from the street, please give generously to the homeless. There have been poor and homeless people throughout history and if we can help them in some small way, as human beings, we should.

Your loving sister,

Henrietta

IF YOU SEE SOMETHING, SAY SOMETHING

Traveling from Cleveland to Hartford, I couldn't help but observe the pen-and-ink drawings the guy sitting next to me was rapidly scratching onto his drawing pad. Non-stop, he crafted one drawing after another, seemingly obsessed and in a drawing trance for the entire flight. They were all quite gruesome, disturbing, sexually charged images of ragged, scrawny, and almost naked women in unnatural and uncomfortable positions, falling over each other, each manifesting great pain and fear.

An athletic type, this guy was probably in his mid-fifties with pinkish skin, a freshly shaved head, and a gold earring. He made no attempt to hide his disturbing sketches.

"Perhaps," I thought, "it's because he just likes this sort of dark stuff and likes to shock people around him. Or perhaps it's a cry for help." I figured that, as a man with a wife and daughters, I had a right to be concerned and - no - I didn't have an overactive imagination. I knew what I saw. However, when I got off the plane, daily life took over and the incident shifted to the back burner.

It had been eleven months since the last young woman had disappeared from our area and residents were once again getting jittery, dreading the news that some stranger - or worse, someone they knew - could be the next victim. Everyone hoped that this yearly nightmare had run its course and that those responsible may already be in jail for other crimes, or dead.

One day, at dusk, on the way to Hartford airport to pick up a friend, I passed the Connecticut tobacco wrapper fields and barns and had a flashback to the drawings by that man on the plane. I realized that the background in his drawings was very similar to the long rows of shaded tobacco structures in the foreground, and the barns looked very similar to the ones I now saw. Since I was early for my friend's flight, I pulled off the highway onto a local road and meandered through the area, taking pictures of the buildings and fields. When I returned home, I converted the color images to black and white and printed them out. Sure enough, they looked remarkably similar to the pen-and-ink drawings made by the bald stranger.

So, what did I really know? Not much and I feared that my imagination was running wild. I considered going to the police. "What I know for sure," I pondered, "is that I sat next to a man making weird, disturbing drawings. It's a remote possibility that the tobacco plantations were the back-drop for each of those drawings, and perhaps a clue to the mysterious disappearance of all of those women."

I also realized that each of the victims was, according to public record, probably abducted within a twenty-mile radius of the tobacco fields. It was a long shot and I questioned my motivation, thinking that maybe what I wanted was to be the hero that solved this mystery.

As the weeks passed, doing nothing weighed heavily on my conscience. It was almost a year since the last girl had disappeared and it was very likely that another one would be abducted this month and never heard from again; and I was not taking any action. Part of me thought that, as lame as my theory might be, it was more than the police had. And since

I knew this guy's name - from the boarding pass he dropped when deplaning that I just happened to pick up to use as a bookmark for the book I had just started - I had something that they didn't.

So, I decided to do a bit of sleuthing of my own on the weekends, meticulously reviewing the archives of the local newspapers and the YouTube interviews with the bereaved families, friends, and teachers of the victims. I was looking for a common thread, but there was none. The fact that each of the young, attractive women was between fifteen and eighteen - and lived in the greater Hartford area - was not clue enough. I had a theory and I knew that man's identity; this could be helpful to the police, but only if he was actually the culprit.

"Could I save a life?" I thought. "Could I save many girls' lives in the future and find closure for the families of the twelve women who disappeared over the last twelve years?" I felt like I was on a mission and had an obligation to say and do *something*.

Before work, on a raw and rainy Monday morning, I drove to the police station to tell my story. I had with me the guy's boarding pass, the pictures I had taken of the tobacco fields, and the home addresses of each of the twelve victims.

Slowly, I walked up the familiar, stained cement steps of the police station, feeling the weight of anticipated rejection and expecting to be laughed right out the door.

The stale smell of the police station brought me back to my youth and an incident in high school when a disgruntled ex-girlfriend accused me of raping her. It did get a lot of attention back then for a few weeks, and I'm sure that it's memorialized. My mug shot and fingerprints may still be on file here. Thankfully, in the end, the girl recanted her story. She was upset with me because I started to date her best friend behind her back. She confessed her evil deed to her priest, who convinced her to come clean and not destroy an innocent person's life. But still, this weighed heavily on me then and now, and I still have nightmares of being taken from my home late at night, sitting in the back of the patrol car, handcuffed, while the sharp metal cuffs pinned behind me caused great pain as they cut into my wrists. I rubbed my wrists, remembering the pain.

That was many years ago and I've been leery of the law ever since because they tend to believe the accuser in a rape case and it's not always 'innocent until proven guilty', as we are led to believe. I know that each one of the police officers I came in contact with looked at me like it could have been their daughter and that 'this creep probably did rape her'.

I was sweating heavily, shivering from the raw weather, and thinking I should just turn around and leave. The dingy lights, faded green walls, and creepy looking individuals sitting on a bench close by - along with my distasteful memories - were enough to make anyone turn and run. I looked up at the grey-haired Sergeant sitting several feet above me on his intimidating perch. He was on the phone. I stood looking up at him, waiting for recognition, and I gleaned from his conversation that it was a personal call with a friend, planning a weekend getaway. He was totally immersed in the call and didn't notice me, as he swiveled from side to side in his big leather chair, first toward the police blotter and then to the patrolman's roster on the wall.

I didn't know the protocol here and, after a few minutes of standing awkwardly waiting for his acknowledgment, I tried to get his attention by waving when he swiveled in my direction; but he was at that moment looking up to the ceiling. The longer I waited, the more convinced I was that this duty officer would not be the right person to speak with.

I fast-forwarded my theory and could see him leaking the information to the press and taking credit for this new lead; in fact, if my theory was correct, possibly unwittingly giving the abductor the opportunity to get out of town to commit his crimes somewhere else.

Finally, he told the person he was speaking to 'hold on', seeming a little annoyed that I was standing there so long and distracting him from his conversation. He asked me in a deep, condescending, drill-sergeant tone: "What can I do for you, kid?" taking me by surprise. Without knowing why, I said the words "You look busy, sir. I'll come back a little later." I turned and walked out of the building as quickly as I could.

"I am a damn chicken, a coward," I thought, as I walked down the precinct steps. The shivering had stopped and the nausea had subsided; I felt as if I made the right choice. I realized that what I needed to do now would be to call the FBI. "Yes, that's what I'll do when I have a few quiet minutes at the end of the day. I won't give them details on the phone," I thought. "I'll make an appointment to see them as soon as possible."

The very next day, without calling first, I went to the F.B.I. office and spoke to a Mr. Smith (really!). He was listening to me with half an ear at first, flipping through some papers on his desk, so I had a feeling that he considered me just another crackpot with a useless lead. However, after a few minutes, when telling him about the tobacco fields, I suddenly had his full attention. Apparently, there was now a connection between my report and that of a woman who had a similar theory. In fact, she was also on a flight months earlier, also traveling into Hartford from Cleveland, and also sat next to a man sketching in the same way. Since she worked near the tobacco fields, she recognized the buildings.

Her description of the man was the same as mine. However, I had something she didn't; I had his boarding pass.

Officer Smith asked if I would sit with an artist and attempt to create a picture of this person. The officer told me that the woman had already helped to create a picture; I asked if I could see it. He said that it would be best if I didn't, because it may influence my description. I spent about an hour with the artist and tried to remember as many details as possible; but sitting next to the man on the plane, I didn't really get a good frontal view of his face. It turned out that the woman did get a good frontal view of the man.

After I completed my description, I was shown the picture that was rendered with the woman's description; it was clear to everyone that this was the same man. It gave me the shivers. Next, the two images were used to create a three-dimensional rendering of the man's face. When this was done, it was sent to the local police department near the tobacco fields. The police showed the picture around to people that worked at several of the tobacco farms, and a few said it looked like a truck driver that delivered fertilizer from time to time.

Mr. Smith - having been involved in the last three missing-women investigations - decided to look into the man whose name I had from his boarding pass. They found out that he was indeed a truck driver, delivering fertilizer and other chemicals to the tobacco fields on a weekly basis. They decided to tail him. Weeks went by and they didn't observe any unusual behavior.

The guy had a wife and two teenage sons, and he went home each night after his truck run. He had no record, not even a traffic violation. Just when they felt they were at a dead end, the man drove to the airport one morning and flew out to Cleveland. Once he was on the plane, the F.B.I.

contacted their office in Cleveland and, when he deplaned, he was followed to a private home where, as it turned out, he had *another* wife and family.

So now the F.B.I. in Hartford decided to ask for a search warrant for the man's home in Hartford, citing bigamy, but telling the judge that he was actually a suspect in the Hartford area serial abductions; the search warrant was quickly granted.

The man's wife in Hartford was devastated by the news of her husband's deceptive double life. She told the F.B.I. that he traveled every month or two on business and was usually gone for a week each time. They could not tell her that her husband was a suspect in far more serious crimes. They searched the home from top to bottom, and the garage and the grounds, and came up with nothing. As they were leaving the garage, one of the officers snagged his coat button on a large fishing net hanging on the wall.

As one of the officers helped him remove the net from his uniform button, he noticed something that looked like blood. They looked at each other and, wondering, went back in the house and asked the man's wife what he used the net for. She told him that, once a year, her husband and two of his friends would take off for a few days and go to Boston fishing. They would use the net to catch fish, so it was likely fish blood.

The officer asked when they went on their Boston trip the previous year and she looked it up. It happened to be the exact week of the last abduction. They asked who the two friends were, and she gave their names and addresses. The wife also told them that, for ten or twelve years, they went on the same fishing trip at about the same week each year.

They took the net to the lab and discovered that the blood was human blood; but once again hit a dead end, because they had no victims to check DNA against.

Suspicion was mounting and one of the most disturbing facts for me was that one of the truck driver's fishing companions was the very same police sergeant that I was going to tell my theory to. It turned out that the third person was the owner of one of the tobacco farms.

When the suspect returned from Cincinnati, he was apprehended for questioning - as were the other two men, whose homes were also searched. In the sergeant's home, there was a bottle of chlorophyll hidden in the attic. In the other man's home, they uncovered video cards in a hidden compartment in his desk, with all the proof they needed to convict the three of multiple counts of kidnapping, rape, torture, and murder.

When the videos were played, they showed the gruesome way these men raped, killed, and dismembered their innocent young victims for their personal entertainment. All three confessed and gave up the hidden, underground spots in the tobacco field where the women's remains were found.

So, if you see something, say something. You may save a life and it may even be someone you know or love.

JOHNNY BE GOOD

It was 1970. I sat in my metallic blue, 1955 Olds '88 convertible, top down, directly in front of the Frick Museum on Madison Avenue and 36th Street in Manhattan, taking in the towering buildings and the warm sun of late spring. On the radio was Chuck Berry belting out 'Johnny Be Good'.

Three men in black suits, black ties, and blinding white shirts approached my car. Two were tall and lanky, one short and muscular, all appearing to be stereotypical plain-clothesmen. Their lack of expression, erect posture, and bulges in their jackets gave me the creeps.

It seemed like a bit of overkill to have three undercover cops come to tell me that I was parked illegally and had to move - or was it my noisy muffler that I'd been planning to fix for weeks? They kept their distance at first, looked at my front license plate, and lingered until a fourth man in black arrived, looked at the plate and nodded "Yes" to the others.

Two of the men approached and the others left. "Theodore Schmidt?" one politely inquired.

I nodded 'yes' and asked, "What did I do?" I was told by the short one that they knew that I wanted to make 'a past wrong, right'. "That's a relief," I said to myself, "whatever the hell they were talking about."

They told me what the 'wrong' was and how they could help fix it, if I agreed. I didn't have to think long and agreed.

The two men got into my car and we headed out of the city to the prep school I attended in New England years earlier. Even though I was way past my high school days, I always wanted to go back and right a wrong, even though I knew that it was really impossible. It was too late, I thought. It was uncanny that they knew about it since I had never told anyone. The event in question still haunted me and always replayed vividly in my memory.

At the end of that school year of 1957, the sophomore class took off to Martha's Vineyard and Nantucket on a school trip. We all loaded into the school's bus and headed east toward Cape Cod. Many hours later we boarded a ferry from Woods Hole to Martha's Vineyard. We rented bikes at the port and, in twenty minutes of pedaling, were at a hostel a few miles from the airport. We checked in quickly, found bunks, dropped our backpacks, and biked to the cafeteria at the airport, the only place open for dinner.

When we arrived at the airport, LaRue - one of our teachers and our chaperone - realized that she had left her wallet back at the hostel. Since I had led the pack to the airport, she figured I was the fastest and asked me if I would mind returning to the hostel to retrieve her wallet. I felt that I was on an 'important mission' because no one could have dinner until I returned. I was so pleased that she chose me, especially since I had a crush on this beautiful French woman ten years my senior.

As I started back from the hostel to the airport, I realized that I could cut the trip in half by cutting across the runway instead of circumventing the entire airport. There were no planes approaching and I just assumed, for no logical reason, that there would be no more planes landing that evening. So I pedaled - carefree - down the unpaved runway approach. Suddenly, seemingly out of nowhere, a plane approached behind me - directly in my path - and I ducked down between the handlebars, the wheels of the plane just missing my head by a few inches. In the dim light of dusk, the pilot didn't see me until it was too late for him to take evasive action.

In hindsight, at that point, I should have aborted my mission, turned around and taken the longer route on the road back to the airport arrivals building. But I knew that everyone was waiting for my return and, perhaps feeling a big responsibility to get to the cafeteria as soon as possible - and be a hero of course - I figured that I could make it before another plane arrived. I looked around the sky and there did not appear to be any planes in sight so I got back on my bike and raced down the runway as fast as I could.

The reception I received was not pretty - and not the one I expected. For sure, it was not one for a hero, but for a stupid fool who should have known better than to ride a bike down an active runway, especially after a close call with a landing plane.

The pilot had already exited the plane, letting LaRue know what happened. When I coasted up the tarmac like a returning hero, I was accosted by a screaming pilot calling me a stupid fool (which I must admit now, I was) and LaRue also screaming at me, almost in tears, as the students laughed in the background. I was confused. I was mortified.

Until that moment, I hadn't realized that it was a very close call for me. LaRue was understandably very upset, because I could have been killed and, since she had sent me on the mission, I'm sure she would have felt forever responsible for returning to the school with one less student.

LaRue continued screaming, asking why I had done such a foolish thing. I felt trapped, my actions misunderstood, still rationalizing my decision to take the shortcut and get back to the airport quickly so everyone could have dinner.

LaRue was the school's French and German teacher. She continued screaming, "Do you realize you could have gotten killed?" I guess I reached my breaking point and lashed out with: "Shut up, you nigger!" - words that I had never used before when speaking to a black person. I couldn't believe I said them but, at the moment, I was just blindly defending myself, considering her and everyone else ungrateful for my good intentions. I was not a hero; I was a fool.

I saw the hurt on LaRue's face as she stopped yelling and said not another word to me. LaRue grew up in France where there was little or no prejudice, so she was really shocked. I can now, so many years later, still see the hurt in her face. I could not take back what I said. I told her later that I was sorry, but she turned and walked away, and would not speak to me. She never spoke to me again and her boyfriend - our history teacher and ski instructor, who I was friendly with and who taught me to ski - also gave me the cold shoulder for the rest of the semester.

When we returned to school, LaRue told Hans - the headmaster and school founder - about the airport incident. Soon thereafter, Hans came to my room, told me how disappointed he was at the way I spoke to LaRue, and said it went against all his and the school's principles as a multiracial school with students from around the world. He told me that, as a punishment, I would not be allowed to go to the stables or ride the horses; something that he knew I enjoyed very much.

Weeks later, when I was home for the summer, my parents received a letter informing them that I could not return the next year; to my relief, they were not told exactly why. My parents questioned me and I told them that I was having trouble keeping up and my grades were bad. I never did tell them what happened. I never told anyone.

All those years since, I wished I could take it back, erase that moment in time - but the damage was done. Hans was very progressive and way ahead of his time as an educator. His stress on equal rights and equality for women was monumental, and we all basked in the warmth of respect for him and each other, regardless of our background.

That was 1957, a time of racial turmoil and tension in the United States. It was the time of major school desegregation objectives, school bussing, equal rights in restaurants, public transportation, public restrooms, hotels, bars, and attempts by the government to break up the KKK and rid America of their evil white supremacy agenda. It was the time of Martin Luther King, of Malcolm X, of Rosa Parks and much more - but not all Americans, especially those in the Deep South, were trying to find a higher moral ground. Many wanted the status quo and were still fighting the Civil War; they felt deep resentment that they could no longer have their own slaves to abuse.

Earlier that year, at a student-teacher meeting, Hans suggested that the student body finance an exploratory trip to Selma, Alabama. It consisted of a white woman and a black man, both seniors. In hindsight - because of the future killings of Schwerner, Goodman and Chaney by the KKK in 1964 and the assassination of Dr. King, in April of 1968 - it was an extremely dangerous trip for them to make, but no one really knew how dangerous it was or they would not have been allowed to go.

They were away for a week and, when they returned, they told us what they saw and experienced in vivid detail. It was not a pretty sight and it looked like Dr. Martin Luther King Jr. and other black leaders that led the marches for equal rights would experience a long, painful, and dangerous uphill battle for equality in America.

We were young and impressionable and I'd say that looking back, we were all blueprinted by Hans' values of *equality for all*. I would say that he molded us into a very special group of people that went forth into the world to promote equality.

During the three-hour drive to my old school, I told the men in black all about my time at the school and the incident that I always regretted.

With the two men in black, I entered the building where I had lived as a student. It was now a co-ed dorm and I would share a room with two boys of fifteen. I explained to them that my parents wanted me to finish up. It was a joke; they didn't get it. I pulled my duffle bag into the room. One of the boys had a small record player with Chuck Berry belting out 'Johnny Be Good'.

In reality, it was 1981 and I had been lying on the sandy beach as some guy with a boom box walked by blasting out 'Johnny Be Good', which woke me from my dream and took me back to reality.

And now, years later, I believe I understand why I lashed out at sweet LaRue. One day, before I was born, my grandmother - still a young woman - was walking down the subway steps in Manhattan. She was stopped on the stairs by two black men. They ordered her at knifepoint to give them her money. She refused and when one tried to grab her bag, she pulled it up to her chest. This saved her life because the other man at that moment attempted to stab her in the heart. She was lucky, the bag saved her life, but she was bitter and every black person after that was a 'nigger' and a 'killer'.

She held the grudge all her life. I remember her whispering under her breath when she looked out her window at home as a black person walked by in her all-white neighborhood: "Another nigger - what is he doing here?"

I cannot think of any other reason for my outburst that dark day as a teenager on the island of Martha's Vineyard so many years ago.

LaRue, wherever you are, I am truly sorry.

MORNING GLORY

"Farm life," I thought, as I sipped my second cup of coffee and considered how each day on the farm was much the same routine and the only divergence was church on Sunday, a state fair once a year, Thanksgiving, and Christmas. We never really had a vacation where we could go away and experience other cultures and scenery, because the cows needed to be milked and fed, and the chickens needed to be tended - as well as the other animals that depended on us one hundred percent.

However, there was a day, just ten years ago today, that was different than all the others in my life. It was fall and the beginning of the harvest. I walked from the farmhouse down the stone path, the purple-and-white morning glories clinging to the stone wall were wide open, and the roosters were making themselves known as they prowled the hencoop. The cows, bells ringing, were headed through the silver gate to the south pasture.

As I walked through the rows of rhubarb to decide if today should be the first day of the harvest, I tripped over a stone, lost my balance, and went flying between the furrows of the two-foot-high fully mature plants.

At twenty-five, I was in excellent health and physical shape, but - for some reason - I could not get back up on my feet. Something invisible seemed to be holding me fast to the ground. By ten o'clock, without the protection of my wide brim hat that gone flying with my fall and rested somewhere between the rhubarb furrows, the sun's strong rays in the cloudless sky started to burn my face. I became weaker by the minute, fighting the urge to faint.

I always returned to the farmhouse after a few hours for my third cup of coffee and a slice of my sister Sue's chocolate-raisin pound cake or her amazing cookies. She won many blue ribbons over the years at the state fair for her cookies. Three hours later, I heard Sue calling my name with concern in her voice. I called out to her, but my voice was weak and - with the wind blowing away from her and blocked by the large rhubarb leaves - she did not hear me or see me, as I waved frantically.

A few minutes later, I felt something rough and wet moving across my cheeks, my eyes, and my forehead, and when I opened my burning lids - to my great pleasure - saw my dog Honeycup. As she licked, she whined for a few minutes, but when I didn't get up, she sensed I was in trouble and started to bark and howl as I've never seen or heard her carry on before.

Fortunately, it caught the attention of Jim, my friend and neighbor just to the south. I felt relieved as I saw him approach, but lost consciousness and was woken by the stinging pain of a needle going into my arm. As Doctor Frank was slowly removing the needle he said, "You will be fine, sonny boy. I'm just giving you some painkiller for the third-degree burns on your face and neck. Please stay in bed today and I will return to see you tomorrow morning. Agreed?"

Reluctantly, anxiously, I agreed. Anxious because I knew the harvest must begin, the cows milked, the chickens fed and their eggs gathered, as well as all the other daily farm chores that needed my attention. I knew that Sue could not handle all this on her own.

I rested for several days and, each day, nearby farmers came by to help Sue with the daily chores in the morning and returned in the early evening, after they had their dinner, to help milk our cows. This is what farm people do: they are always there for each other. It was part of our farm culture. We all looked after each other in times of stress, need, and tragedy.

After a few days, I felt strong enough to venture out and I decided to revisit the spot where I tripped and fell. There was something mysterious and unsettling about that fall, and about my inability to get back on my feet. For several days, while in bed and on the couch, I stared at the ceiling, searching over and over for answers.

When I came across the rock that I had tripped over, I wedged it out of the ground to make sure that neither I nor anyone else would trip over it in the future. To my surprise, I discovered two very strange, nut-like objects that must have been under the rock for a long time. They were oval in shape, a little over an inch in length, with small, protruding orange stems. The objects were dark grey with small, purple specks that seemed to sparkle and glow as if there were some energy or life form inside of them. Carefully, I removed each, placed them in my handkerchief and brought them back to the farmhouse.

Over the next few days, many of my friends and neighbors dropped in to see how I was feeling. Word of the strange objects traveled fast in the hamlet and some folk came to see them in person. Each visitor gingerly ran them through their fingers in wonderment and placed them back on my handkerchief.

Most people just scratched their heads, having no clue as to what they were touching and looking at. Most were farmers, some trained in horticulture, who - through the generations - were very much in touch with rock and plant formations in the area. One man speculated that it could be a seed mutation of some kind. Kidding around, another farmer said, "maybe it's from outer space" and everyone had a good laugh.

Farmer Green, the oldest person in our hamlet having just celebrated his 94th birthday, decided to pay us a visit on hearing about the strange nuts. He came with the help of Seth and Roger, his grandsons who ran the family farm.

Farmer Green picked up one of the objects and, like the others before him, gingerly rotated it with his fingers. Even though his sight was failing, the unusual suede-like texture immediately had him sitting up at attention. It was clear that he was disturbed and a bit uncomfortable with these little nuggets. After examining both of them, he placed them back on the table and asked everyone come sit at the table with him, because he had something to tell us.

I poured him a whiskey, which he wasted no time in consuming, extending his glass for another. He told us that he knew about the objects. He asked me to go to my 'new-fangled machine', meaning my computer, and look up UFO sightings, Hampton County, Oregon, June 12, 1931.

I did as he asked and quickly found a news story on the event. He asked that I read it out loud, so I did, and it went like this:

"At about five AM, on the morning of June 12, 1931, as the farmers in Hampton County Oregon, town of Hillside, were heading to their fields, they reported the sighting of a strange bluish and orange glowing object in the sky in the shape of a large bullet. It made no discernable sound, but the dogs in the area all started to bark, and the chickens and crows became silent. It hovered over some of their farms and dropped many glowing, nut-shaped objects into the fields. There were some thirty-five sightings by adult men, six women, and several young boys who were in the fields with their fathers. They each reported that this large object stayed over their field for about minute and then just *disappeared*. Little else is known about the extraterrestrial visit. Farmer Green told us that, when the Air Force personnel arrived, they swore the residents to secrecy, concerned that if others found out about the event it could cause a national panic. And then many UFO watchers and newspaper reporters from around the country - and around the world - would converge on their peaceful little hamlet."

After I read this, Farmer Green proceeded to describe the events. He told us that all of the farmers had been ordered by Air Force personnel to help locate all the nut-like objects, (about a thousand in total were found) and, under the supervision of an officer, ordered to make a great bonfire on his farm where the objects were all tossed in. At first, when they hit the fire, they glowed white, then red, then purple, and then just... disappeared!

Farmer Green was the last person alive to know about these strange objects. Everyone else from his era had taken the secret to their graves. Had two of these objects not been unearthed now, the secret would have gone to the grave with the last living witness.

So, if there was ever any doubt that intelligent life existed elsewhere in the galaxies, the proof sat on a kitchen table of a farmhouse in Hillsdale, Oregon.

TALK OF THE TOWN

Sixteen, and possessing marginal confidence, Jane stepped from her home in a middle-class bedroom community and walked quickly toward Joe's waiting convertible. It was a typical hot rod, sporting dull grey primer paint and a purposely loud and annoying muffler. She pulled the squeaky door open, smiled at Joe and hopped in, looking around for the seat belt and finding the rarely-used buckle buried between the badly stained terrycloth seat covers.

Joe, his mouth now ajar in disbelief, silently lipped "seatbelt?" in serious annoyance at her lack of trust in his driving. He was rumored to drive fast and reckless, and had several very close calls... so she heard from friends, who warned her against stepping into his 'deathtrap'.

They exchanged short "hi-hi" greetings with flash on-and-off smiles and were off on their first date. Her neck snapped back as he pushed the gas pedal to the floor, rapidly shifting into second then third gear, tires screeching, leaving black rubber lines in the road for all to observe how cool he was. Jane, slightly more mature and far more sensible, thought, "Is this a mistake?" as she bit her upper lip again and again. Pointing to the radio, she broke the awkward silence and asked, "May I?"

He responded with a condescending, "Sure, babe," and she commenced surfing for her favorite songs.

Unrealistic, desperate and naïve, Jane had convinced herself that she needed the exposure by going out and being seen with the ever-cool and ever-popular Joe. She was dying to be invited into a certain clique at school and that night may be her ticket in. "He's cute," she thought, "but what's that smell?" She wondered with some consternation, "Maybe it's leaking gas or maybe it's the popular (rumored aphrodisiac) English Leather fragrance."

After a few minutes, they picked up Betty and Frank at a local corner hang-out. They'd been going steady for about a month, and the locker room talk was that there was more than petting going on. Jane thought to herself, "They're cool, real cool, and I'm gonna be seen with these guys around town tonight, and tomorrow everyone in school will be talkin' about me!" She thought, "I'll be the talk of the town." However, she was getting bad vibes from Joe's arrogance, his reckless, show-off driving, and the smell, which she realized was alcohol.

The two couples made the rounds, stopping first at the Mobil on route 46 and Country Road. Ken, one of Joe's pals, was working as a mechanic's apprentice on the swing shift. When he heard Joe's distinctive loud muffler, he took a break - still full of grease - for a smoke, to shoot the breeze with his friend, and to check out and flirt with the girls.

Next stop was the Texaco station on Walton Road, where Joe put a buck's worth of gas in the car. He then headed to the White Castle, where young chicks took orders from the cars' occupants and secured a large serving tray outside the driver's window. All the girls working there knew Joe because he was a regular and always showed up with a different chick.

The two couples made small talk and gulped down the wafer-thin, square burgers - greasy and very tasty. Joe hit the horn briefly for the waitress to bring the check. He looked at it quickly, held it up high and announced to the occupants, "Two bucks each and that includes a tip."

It was eleven and Jane had an eleven-thirty curfew... or else! But her fear of looking uncool would override her common sense, and her promise to her mom that she would be home on time. She kept silent.

Since she had informed Joe earlier of her curfew, she hoped that he was bringing her home, but she quickly realized that he had other plans: a joy ride and then on to a well-known make-out spot.

It was a dark road with few curves, deserted at that hour, and very tempting for speed - especially when alcohol was in charge. Add loud, fast music pumping everyone up and a powerful, supercharged engine with 250 big ones under the hood dying to show off their muscle, and you have an invitation for trouble. "Great," she thought. "Alcohol *and* speed - what a deadly combination. I'm too young to die!"

Adrenaline raced through the car's occupants, the invincible four now hurtling forward into the dark, faster and faster. The engine, in high-pitch overdrive, was begging for more gas and air to flow through the oversized four-barrel carburetor. The hi-beams couldn't light the road in front of them fast enough at that speed, and Jane's eyes were riveted to the speedometer: 60, 70, 80, 90, and climbing.

She was scared to death and, at the same moment, high from the rush of speed and music, reassuring herself over and over again, "It's worth it. Tomorrow I'll be the talk of the town. I'm with the cool crowd now!" She was fully caught up in the moment, her fears subsided and she started to enjoy the rush.

The junk heap vibrated and swayed as it sped dangerously over the blacktop like a speedboat floating almost out of control over choppy waters. But this was not water and there were trees all around.

A large yellow sign came up quickly at one hundred miles an hour: **WARNING - SLOW DOWN sharp curve ahead.** But Joe was looking in the rear-view mirror for recognition from his pals. He never saw the warning sign and, when he turned his eyes back to the road, an ember from the cigarette hanging from his lips caught the wind and fell between his legs. He looked down and, in that split second of incredibly poor judgment and impaired reflexes, he chose death for all.

Fast forward to tomorrow. Jane, Joe, and the couple in the back seat are now *the talk of the school* and *the talk of the town*. Four sets of parents have spent sixteen years responsibly raising and sacrificing for their precious children with the hopes and dreams shared by all caring parents.

Three days later, parents, siblings, family, friends, teachers, the press, the mayor, and clergy participate at a surreal and heartbreaking funeral ceremony as four soon-to-be-adults, with expectations of 'a full life', are now - one by one - lowered into the graves that they should not have known for a half century or more. Four families will never ever be the same; robbed by the innocence and ignorance of youth. No graduation, no marriage, no grandchildren, no happy tomorrow.

After the service, as everyone walks to their cars, Ken - Joe's pal from the garage - is first to depart and climb into his souped-up auto. He starts it at once and immediately pushes the accelerator to the floor, again and again, revving up the engine so all can hear. He grinds the gears into first, tires squeal; then into second, tires squeal again; and into third, tires screeching and squealing disrespectfully all the way out of the cemetery, leaving black tracks in the pavement for all to witness his departure.

With grief of his own, he is now defiant of death and speeds away, trying to distance himself from reality.

An important lesson for Ken? No lesson for Ken. He too, in his mind, is invincible. That is, until the day he takes three others prematurely to their graves - two being innocent kids in another car. Ken would have his turn in small-town America as *the talk of the town*.

THE FOUR-CARAT DIAMOND PENDANT

It was a blind date and I was nervous as hell because the girl could have been a dog. Besides, I was set up by a coworker of my father's, so I needed to make a good impression. Up until then, blind dates were always like bad dreams.

She lived in an apartment building in Queens, some two miles from where I lived with my parents. It wasn't just any old apartment building; this was a new, luxury high-rise with a covered circular driveway, a smartly uniformed doorman, and a posh lobby.

The receptionist, decked out in a dapper, military-style uniform, looked down at me from his marble perch and politely asked, "How may I help you, son?" He rang up to the apartment to announce my arrival and signaled me to follow him to the elevators. He pointed to an elevator where the door was open, ushered me in, placed a key into the panel under the word PENTHOUSE, turned the key, and removed it. He informed me very politely, "It's the door on the right, young man. 15H. Have a nice day."

The elevator was unlike anything I'd ever been in: plush red carpet, antique mirrors, an oiled stainless-steel door, and the buttons were body heat-activated little red touchpads. "Very cool," I thought.

There was a rush of acceleration as the elevator - smooth and quiet - lifted me to the penthouse floor in a matter of seconds and then, a blood-rushing break and soft stop. The doors opened and, behold, a beautiful, young woman was waiting for me, framed in the doorway of 15H. She held out her hand. "Hello, Ted," she said softly in a beautiful French accent. "I am Ariana. Did you find the building easily?"

"Yes," I said. "I know this area well."

I followed her down a long hallway covered with a beautiful, silk oriental runner. The hallway walls were adorned with pictures in gilded frames, all of well-dressed people with a jockey on a horse in the winner's circle at a racetrack. In the pictures, the men sported wide-brim fedoras and linen suits, the elegant women were mostly in linen, sporting hats adorned with artificial flowers, fruits, feathers, ribbons, and tulle.

I followed Adriana into the living room. She was wearing a short, tight, black sheath dress that showed off all her curvaceous attributes. Her olive skin and beautiful face glowed with youth, and her jet-black hair and deliciously less-than-innocent cleavage were hard to avoid.

The penthouse apartment had an unusually high ceiling for an apartment, and the living room was huge. All the outside walls were sliding doors leading out to a wrap-around terrace with panoramic views of the white marble courthouse across the boulevard, framed by the eastern end of Flushing Meadow Park. I could see planes making their approach into La Guardia airport.

I was taken aback by the almost life-size bronze of a muscular Arabian racehorse in motion, all legs pulled high to the belly, appearing suspended as if it were straining to cross the finish line first.

Ornate crystal chandeliers sparkled in the living and dining rooms. Porcelain figurines were placed on Louis IV carved gold-adorned tables and settees. Large green, red and gold-leaf Chinese vessels sat like sentinels on the ends of sofas and loveseats upholstered in intricately detailed red and emerald jacquard designs, with gold tassels running along their skirts. The gold-threaded silk curtains, decorated in ornate swags and jabots, represented window treatment affordable by only the very wealthy. All the furniture had been smuggled out of Morocco, all having been in their home in Casablanca.

This was the way the wealthy Sephardic Jews had lived in Tangiers and Casablanca before the mass exodus to Israel, Europe and the Americas that began after the Six-Day War with Israel and its Arab neighbors. These were the same Jews that were cast out of Spain in 1481 and now, after building a life and becoming part of the fabric of Morocco, because they were Jews, they had to yet again move or face persecution... or worse. The Arab nations all attacked little Israel and, because they lost miserably and were sore losers, actually had the nerve to blame the Israelis for saving their little nation and winning the war!

Ariana asked me to make myself comfortable and that her mother would like to meet me. I sunk into one of the three plush sofas and nervously waited. Her mother - a large, imposing, elegant, and beautiful woman - rolled herself out in a wheelchair. She was adorned in gold bracelets and a large diamond necklace. I felt as though I was meeting royalty.

I could see the mother-daughter resemblance. I remembered the pictures in the hallway and realized that the mother, now much older, was the young, elegant woman in the winner's circle, along with Ariana's father. I understood then that those racehorses were theirs. Wow! They owned Arabian racehorses!

Her mother spoke little English and asked Ariana in

French to ask me if I would like some Moroccan mint tea. Alice translated her question to me. I really didn't want hot tea on a very hot day, but I didn't want to appear unsociable, so I said, "Sure, I would like that." To this day, I can remember the smell of the fresh mint, its cool taste, and the way it pleasantly numbed my tongue and lips.

It was a beautiful Sunday in August. We approached my convertible and I asked Ariana if she would like the top down; her face lit up, she loved the idea. We drove a short distance to Flushing Meadow Park. We walked along the bank of the large pond where people of all ages were floating their model sailboats and remote-controlled powerboats, while others were slowly, aimlessly rowing around in rented rowboats.

I thought to myself, "Wow, she's a very nice girl, so refined - maybe too refined for me. A real beauty!" I took an immediate liking to her and everything about her. We stopped at the food concession by the boat ramp and watched all the activity on and around the pond, engaged in small talk, and nibbled on hot dogs, slowly sipping iced tea from a paper cup.

I discovered that she liked American music, so that became a big part of our conversation and, of course, she told me about her life in Morocco and the difficult transition to the United States - and the loss of her father. He had died two years earlier of a heart attack, shortly after they moved to America - probably, she supposed, because he was seriously overweight and a heavy smoker.

I thought that she liked me because she held onto my arm while we were walking around the lake. I told her that I had been married and divorced, and had a little boy. She knew all about it from her uncle and asked if I had a picture of my son, which of course I did.

It was my first really *nice* blind date and, when I arrived back at her apartment building, she told me that she had a very nice time, thanked me for the hot dog. She said she hoped she would see me again soon and that there was no need to take me upstairs.

I drove away lightheaded, with a vision of that sweet and beautiful young woman dancing in my head. I envisioned going out with her again, thinking about her beautiful face, her calm demeanor, her shiny long black hair, and sensuous, glowing olive skin. I wondered if her mother really approved of me, knowing that I was not a college grad or from a wealthy family. Years later, I realized that my being Jewish was of paramount importance to her mother and was the basis for our first date.

We had a few more dates, even went dancing one night in New York City. I knew she was anxious to meet my parents and I knew that my Mother was dying to meet her. I was very pleased to have a reason to invite her to my home. My Mother was planning a birthday party for her sister on a Sunday afternoon, so if Ariana was available, that was perfect.

At the party, I overheard one of my mother's nosey neighbors admiring the pendant Ariana was wearing. She told the woman that it was a gift from her mother for her eighteenth birthday. The nervy woman asked Ariana if it was a real diamond and, if so, how big it was. It's the kind of thing Jewish women think is appropriate to ask of a total stranger. Alice answered, "It's four carats," seeming a bit surprised at the question.

I realized that the diamond represented more than two years' salary for me, and was larger than anything I'd ever seen or could ever possibly afford if we were ever to get serious. I wanted to see Ariana again, but I hesitated and procrastinated so much that months passed without my calling her. Looking back, I realize that I was truly intimidated by that huge diamond. It represented something way out of my reach and I felt Alice was probably out of my reach as well, and in a much different league; she was likely to find and marry a wealthy, well-educated man.

When I saw Marc, Ariana's uncle, he told me that Ariana really liked me and so did her mother. He inquired if I would be asking her out again. I told him that I was planning to, but I was very busy with my regular job and night school, so it was difficult at the moment. Truth be told, I was having trouble making ends meet and was on a very tight budget. I couldn't afford to take this girl out to places befitting her and her four-carat diamond. I never asked her out again and, for sure, it was the four-carat diamond that made me feel so small. It was a shame because I really liked her.

Some years later, I saw Ariana's uncle and he asked me about my life and my job. I asked how Ariana was and he told me that she had gotten married, was living in Washington D.C., and had a child. By then, I had moved on and had all but forgotten about our brief romance.

I assumed she married someone wealthy and well educated, with a big income or his own business or both, so he would be able to provide for her in the princess lifestyle she had always known growing up in Casablanca.

Marc showed me a picture of the guy she married. He looked overweight with premature balding. The picture strangely showed him looking up at the camera while fitting a woman's foot with a shoe. I asked, "Is that his shoe store?"

Marc replied, "No, he is a salesman in the store."

I was surprised and shocked. "So," I thought, "she married a guy with no money, no better education then I had." The one thing that was different between the two of us was that he wasn't intimidated by a four-carat diamond.

I often wonder how different our lives would have turned out if it were not for that diamond and the foolish, naïve thought that I was not good enough for her.

I could easily afford the diamond now.

Never, ever, sell yourself short.

THE POPE'S VISIT TO BANJA LUKA

June 23, 2003

Fact: A defrocked Roman Catholic priest, Miroslav Filipovic, was the commander of 'Jasenovac', the largest concentration camp in the Balkans during World War II.

Fact: The Ustasha - a revolutionary Croatian fascist, racist, ultranationalist terrorist organization also called the 'Croatian Nazi puppet regime' - were amongst the worst murderers in Europe. In 1941, they embarked on a campaign forcing Orthodox Serbs in Croatia and Bosnia to convert to Catholicism or be killed.

Fact: Alojzije Stepinac, then the Roman Catholic Archbishop of Zagreb - with the apparent approval of the Vatican - welcomed the Nazi occupation and dismemberment of Yugoslavia. In April 1941, Stepinac supported the brutal Ustasha regime headed by Ante Pavelic. He embarked on a campaign of genocide, which resulted in the mass murder of hundreds of thousands of innocent people whose only crime was that they were not Catholic and therefore not in step with the Vatican. Incredibly, many of the massacres were organized and conducted by Croatian Roman Catholic priests.

After the war, the Pope of the Roman Catholic Church was not welcome in Serbia or Yugoslavia. The governments *said* it was because "it would bring back terrible memories for the older generation, who could not forget how the Church sided with the Nazis and Ustasha." In fact, it was mostly a religious issue because, for centuries, the Orthodox Church wanted nothing to do with the Vatican - but especially after the Second World War.

Pope John Paul XXIII was relentless in attempting to heal the wounds of war and, in 2003, the government of Serbia reluctantly agreed to permit the Holy Father to visit. His mission was to ask the non-Catholic Christians, along with the Roma (gypsies) and the Jews, for forgiveness for the disgraceful behavior and crimes of the Catholic Church during the war.

The Holy Father finally arrived in the city of Banja Luka, Republic of Srpska, which is now the Serb part of Bosnia-Herzegovina. He was welcomed by a large crowd. He raised an olive branch and silence blanketed the square; weeping could be heard through the crowd. With tears in his eyes, the Holy Father spoke: "From this city, marked in the course of history by so much suffering and bloodshed, I ask Almighty God to have mercy on the sins committed against humanity, human dignity, and freedom - also by children of the Catholic Church - and to foster in all the desire for mutual forgiveness."

Christina, dressed in a black-hooded frock and looking much older than her sixty-four years, had dreamed about this moment since the news of the Holy Father's visit was announced. In Christina's right hand, she held a heavily tarnished silver frame with a faded sepia photograph of her murdered husband, brother, and son.

She strained for that *glance of a lifetime*, hoping to get a good look at the Holy Father, hoping beyond hope that he would see her and acknowledge her presence. She had gone to church every morning for a month to ask for God's help, so that she may be personally blessed by the Holy Father of the Catholic church, because of all the tragic losses she had suffered by the evil deeds perpetrated so many years ago by 'men of the cloth'; losses as vivid for her as if they had taken place yesterday. She was not Roman Catholic, but she felt that she needed to hear the Pope's apology and to receive his blessing.

Around Christina's neck, she bore the weight of three large ornate gold crucifixes, representing both the Trinity and her own personal trinity: son - husband - brother. She also wore, pinned to her dress, the likeness of the Martyr Christina of Tyre, whose name she bore. She knew the legend of the martyred woman and felt her life reflected many sad and similar tragedies.

After the Pope spoke, he climbed back into the open Pope-mobile. With great excitement and anticipation, Christina waited for the Holy Father's procession to emerge through the massive crowd. From a devout Orthodox family, she grew up believing in miracles, even though all her family had for their faith was a lifetime of misfortune and tragedy. This was her opportunity to experience a miracle and God must have been listening because it actually happened.

It was surreal. For one brief moment, the Holy Father's eyes met hers and a flash of sunlight bounced off his crucifix, momentarily blinding her - piercing her soul - sending waves of emotional trauma through her body. The crowd faded white and silent. She reeled, weak and giddy, sharing an intimate moment in the presence and spirit of the Holy Father.

The event would not bring back her husband or her son or her brother, but it would give her the inner peace that she had craved for so long. She understood that the Pope and the Catholic Church were finally acknowledging and taking responsibility and, for the first time, she felt that the souls of her loved ones had been acknowledged and their premature deaths had not been in vain.

The next morning, while still basking in the joy of her 'out-of-body experience' with the Pope, Christina - crossing a street on her way to church - was run over and killed instantly by a careless truck driver speeding through a stop sign. The blessed woman now joined her husband, her brother, and her son.

That evening at his mosque's call to prayer, devout Muslim Mohammed, the truck driver who ran the stop sign - a good and kind family man with a wife and five young children - asked Allah for forgiveness for accidentally running over and killing the old woman. He prayed for Christina's soul to go to heaven to be with Allah and to experience everlasting life and peace… and he promised Allah never, never, *never* to drive carelessly again.

As the city woke from slumber the next morning, Mohammed stepped into his truck, looked at his watch and said aloud, "Oh Allah, I'm late for work again." He knew his boss would be displeased and quickly started the ignition; with a bit of whining of the starter, the engine came to life. Without a moment's hesitation, he shifted into 'drive' and sped off, never taking his foot off the gas pedal as he raced through stop sign after stop sign, even the one where he took Christina's life the previous morning.

Christina was now history and Mohammed's promise to Allah was also now history.

Another day on Planet Earth.

FROTH OF A NATION

A local coffee house in a wealthy town. With eyes barely open, they arrive. In spring, summer, and fall - and straight through the bitter winter months - they come. When it's not too cold or raining, some choose to sit outside on the wobbly metal chairs with lackluster green wooden slats. They balance their white paper coffee cups on the dented metal tables with twisted underpinnings, challenging the most agile to find a comfortable spot for their knees.

Those that sit outside observe the comings and goings: the healthy and athletic, arriving on bicycle and foot; the old, arriving by car and cane; and the average Joe, arriving in his noisy, dirty and dented pickup with the classic skull-and-crossbones on the cab's dirty back window - a good bet that he's a local tradesman or wannabe from the big city. There are, of course, all the other locals and summer visitors that come for a shot of wake up before heading to work, or who show up after dropping their toddlers off at the preschool.

Many arrive accompanied by their dogs - all sizes, pedigrees, mutts, and many rescues. On the shiny, grey wooden porch, their doggies wait patiently, leashes intentionally and conspicuously dropped without a tether to show the other owners how well trained *their* pets are. The furry pets salivate in anticipation of a morsel of their masters' muffin.

Fashionably sloppy, long-haired, rumpled intellectuals arrive at the same time as their freshly scrubbed, denim-clad, blue-collar coffee pals. Some show up to see and be seen, some to sip coffee and share local news and rumors, some to trash politicians, and some to discuss the latest controversial building code that will make the tradesman's job that much more challenging and time-consuming. Some actually come for the coffee and to engage in all of the above.

Click - click - metal on metal - the barista measures fine ground coffee into the portafilter cup. It's loaded and locked into the ornate Italian espresso machine and, within moments, a fine stream of thick, dark brown liquid dribbles out into the waiting cup. With a powerful twist of the handle, the barista removes the portafilter, turns it upside down, and bangs it hard against a wooden bar, dropping the spent grounds into a waiting trash container.

This coffee shop is the level playing field where adults from all backgrounds meet and find common ground to prove to each other that they are worthy of social intercourse with each other. "We had such great plans last year to..." "When John and I got married, we decided to always have Christmas Eve at our house."

"Look!" she quietly commands, arm outstretched, presenting her child's face on her cell phone screen to the friendly barista, who is preoccupied with fixing her coffee concoction.

A stranger behind her chimes in a shrill voice, muffled and softened by the coffee grinder: "Oh! She is *sooo* cute, how old is she?"

Moments later, the patron notices the extra froth left in the stainless-steel cup, bends over the counter and, with a big smile, softly inquires, "Helen, would you mind adding a bit more of that froth please?"

The pleasing *ssssh* sound of super-heated steamed milk promises the half-awake patron that he or she will soon be face-to-face with their very own early morning fix. The wide-brimmed cup wafts both steam and a rich caffeine aroma, and the patron - as part of their daily ritual - stares into the foamy heart design allowing the cup to sit for a few minutes, anticipating the pleasure to come. At just the right moment, the cup is slowly raised and - for a split second - the pleasant sound of froth bubbles is heard as it coats the upper lip. For a brief moment, with eyes closed, the volume of humanity is turned down low.

Several times a week, different groups of six to eight women in their fifties to eighties - all appearing to be well-educated and well-traveled upper crust types - meet in the back of this coffee shop. The first few to arrive spend five painfully screechy minutes moving tables and chairs around and together for the anticipated arrival of the others, at the expense of those already seated hoping for a blissful moment of silence.

The first to arrive is a tall, skinny brunette wearing a hot pink blouse featuring a large green leaf and clinging black polyester stretch pants. Next is a petite woman in jeans and a too-tight, almost transparent blouse a size too small, pulling open between the buttons. Then a stocky, masculine woman enters sporting a red golf shirt and chinos with a wide, gaudy cowboy belt buckle. Struggling in moments later is a very big woman with a shiny scalp peeking through her thinning bluish hair, wearing a much-too-tight knit dress with wide contrasting bright chartreuse and black horizontal (oh, my God!) stripes accentuating her girth and bulges. Then the birthday girl apparently arrives, likely early seventies, also rather large with a ruddy complexion. She is wearing a life-size print of a bowl of fruit on the front of her sweatshirt, her large breasts now appearing gargantuan as they cast a shadow over the table. My thought at that moment: "What did she see in the mirror this morning, before she bravely ventured out into the world to meet her friends?"

150 miles away at Starbucks. In this upscale New York City bedroom community, local folk float in and out for their expensive customized boutique brew, reciting their orders loud and clear over the chatter: "Tall caramel Snickerdoodle Macchiato with soy and a shot, and also a Grande Vanilla Bean Frappuccino with three scoops of blackberry and an eight-pump drizzle of white mocha, three pumps of toasted coconut and three scoops of matcha powder. And that one is to go."

In the fall - eagerly anticipated by Starbucks worshipers as 'simply divine' – is their signature Pumpkin Spice Latte, copied but, in my humble opinion, not in any way equaled by McDonald's or Dunkin' Donuts.

Sitting in a corner, a man and his teenage son – wearing yarmulkes - intermittently lip sync as the boy practices his haphtarah for his upcoming bar mitzvah and simultaneously slurps loudly through his perfectly un-kosher straw. His father, oblivious to those around him, curls his beard with a forefinger, head bobbing up and down in deep prayer.

Waves of short, tall, old, young, fat and skinny folk march smartly in with a mission: to get in line quickly and get that daily caffeine fix. Once in line, the emails, tweets and phone calls commence. Without using actual words, each of these folks proclaim: "Hey everyone, I CAN AFFORD THIS RIDICULOUSLY OVER-PRICED DRINK with five hundred plus calories!" "Hey, everyone, I've made it! Five bucks to start my day is chump change!" They leave with their drinks and head back to their BMWs, Mercedes, and Lincolns. No pickup trucks or dented old sedans here.

Depending on body language, I've learned to choose carefully who I hold the door for when entering a Starbucks. The self-absorbed, walking with their face buried in their cell phone screen or chatting away, are no-nos. For them, it's a given that someone will hold the door open for them. Without so much as an acknowledgment, they rush past me to the end of the line, not realizing that the considerate door opener's rightful place is in line *in front of them*. Sometimes I may hold the door for someone to test my ability to read their self-absorption level. I'm usually wrong, and I seethe as I wait in line behind them. I know - it's a self-inflicted wound.

The general store in a small blue-collar hamlet. In a small hill-town hamlet, settled in 1777, the store is positioned between the town hall and post office. Friendly ladies dole out sincere morning greetings, local news, and other small talk. Parked outside are rusted Corollas, tradesmen's pickups and dump trucks. You can get a lottery ticket, a cup of dishwater coffee, a sugary, fat-laden donut, a pound of stringy roast beef, a bag of ice, a stick of jerky, and a small bottle of overpriced local maple syrup boiled and bottled just up the road, picked up on impulse by passing souvenir-hungry city folk.

Crusty beige floor tiles - discolored from years of constant use and neglect - tell you that this is a local tradesman stop and redneck hangout where most are blind to the lackluster, dreary and unkempt ambiance. Energy inefficient pink fluorescent lights hum, buzz, and flicker, while refrigerator motors provide a continuous symphony of annoying and distracting knocks and high-pitched sounds of distress. Clearly, the owner is just milking this old cow of a convenience store until it or he 'buys the farm', so to speak.

There are slim pickings on the grimy metal shelves where basic groceries should be. No, there wasn't a recent nor'easter or snowstorm warning; this is the way it always is here - you're unlikely to find many goods associated with a convenience store. They always seem to have ice cream and potato chips, but milk and tomatoes are rarely in stock.

There are three booths with cracked, ripped, lumpy and sunken plastic seating, bandaged badly with duct tape. Greasy plasticized tablecloths cover the chipped and battered Formica table tops of yesteryear. The salt and pepper shakers contain a year's worth of grime in their dented tops. Locals don't even notice all this, but strangers passing through gobble down their overcooked rubbery egg sandwich stuffed with soggy bacon and crusty melted American cheese (that should have been tossed a week ago). How inviting! You can be sure they won't be back.

The coffee is housed in two neat rows of eight pump-your-own dispensers offering both regular and decaf, available both flavored and unflavored; but half of the dispensers are empty and when you bring it to the attention of one of the employees, they always say the same thing: "We were just about to make fresh." Some of the dispensers are so old that pumping for a cup of coffee is like milking a cow. Needless to say, this is not my coffee stop of choice, but since it's on occasion the only one in the direction I'm going in - and I need some coffee - I will lower the bar for this one time.

Another general store at the other end of the same hamlet.
The original location was at a well-traveled fork in the road. It had been there since the 1920s and, as you can imagine, had a long history with the locals. They came in religiously each morning to shoot the breeze over a cup of marginal Java and maybe a custard-filled donut or - if they felt flush - an egg, bacon and American cheese on a roll.

The store had been closed for years when the previous owner could no longer run it. The new owner hired a young, very capable and ambitious woman to be her manager and short-order cook. The new manager decorated the place so it was cheerful and welcoming to all. Her landlady promised her that she would sell the business to her in a few years, if she did well and could pay the agreed price and the lease; and that's just what happened. The manager fixed the place up nicely, improved the menu with great offerings and filled the shelves with things people actually wanted to buy (and it wasn't fish hooks and nightcrawlers).

One day, the landlady who sold the woman the business decided that she wanted the space back to reopen it for herself with a new manager. She did not renew the manager's lease and, without a commitment on the building for at least ten years, the woman was unable to continue with the restaurant business she had purchased.

Being a very determined lady, she bought a large property up the street and - within six months - converted it into a store, much nicer than the original. It now attracts most of her old clients and many new ones. It's bright, fresh, super clean, inviting and decorated with a woman's touch. With few exceptions, she still works long hours. During the week, it's mostly locals, trades people, and retirees who sit at the counter, order and chat. On the weekends in the summer, there are often people waiting outside for a table. It's a destination now and the kids love the wonderful pancakes and other sweet offerings. Personally, I'm addicted to her fried egg, cheese, and Canadian bacon sandwich. Their coffee, not quite Starbucks strength, is good enough.

I guess coffee and convenience shops attract all kinds. On one recent visit, a local man was sitting at the counter - a good 75 pounds overweight, his stomach wedged between the stationary back of the stool and the counter. This lack of room between his stomach and his belly should have sent him a clear message that he needed to cut down on his food intake. It was ten in the morning and the waitress had just dropped in front of him a double hamburger with the works: mustard, mayo, catsup, onions, pickles on a twelve-inch sub roll. He carefully removed the tomato and grabbed half of the sandwich with two hands.

With his mouth open as wide as a hippo, he twisted and squeezed and stuffed the end of the sub into his mouth. As his jaws closed, the condiments mingled and oozed out, down his chin, into his beard, and onto his shirt. One half of this sub would be enough for any hungry human, but as he struggled with the first half, he was already removing the tomato from the second half. He wheezed between bites, a sign to any sensible person that his digestive system was not happy with all of the food being shoveled non-stop into his mouth and sent - barely chewed - down through his esophagus into his already bloated stomach.

He continued in a catatonic state of euphoria until the second half of the sub was gone, oblivious to those around the large horseshoe-shaped counter who couldn't avoid the sight. And if this was not enough for his bloated body, he ordered chocolate pudding with whipped cream! When finished, he scraped the bowl anxiously for a minute, expecting the chocolate pudding to reappear for a second round.

What makes this place so special is the woman that owns it. She has a magnetic personality, is liked by everyone, is a wonderful cook, a practical merchant, and everyone knows that she has earned her success.

America starts the day with coffee. Sometimes an egg sandwich, too.

HUNTINGTON STATION DINER

I boarded the Long Island Railroad and settled in for the one hour and thirty-three-minute trip to my summer job at the Huntington Station Diner out on Long Island.

As the train started to move, I opened my paperback, *A Stone for Danny Fisher* by Harold Robbins. At the time, my friend Judy was reading the same book and we spent much time talking about it. We had a mutual interest in reading and writing. Besides this, I was smitten by her striking beauty and attracted to her wit and bubbly personality. She was very smart and one of just a few Jewish friends. She went on to become a professor of poetry and, I, a businessman.

On some days, the restaurant manager would pick me up at home and we would make the long drive together, listen to the news and make small talk about the people at the diner. Little did I know he was having an affair with my mother and that was very likely the reason I got the summer job. The big news then was the disappearance of a young boy who was missing for several weeks. More than once, when on the road to the diner, I pointed to a wooded area and commented, "I bet they find the kid there." As incredible as it seems, that's exactly where they found the boy's body some weeks later.

I usually arrived at the diner by ten and was greeted by stacks of dirty breakfast dishes. The resident dishwasher was a 'colored' man (that's what African-Americans were called back in the day). He was about forty, tall, lanky, and muscular with salt and pepper hair. He had a distinct odor about him. It wasn't at all pleasant and people noticed it at once, cringed and backed away. The odor seemed to come right out of his skin, but it was probably a combination of poor hygiene and stuff he put on his hair to make it straight and shiny.

Freddy was very conscientious and proud to be the head dishwasher. When he smiled, his whole face lit up, showing off his gold teeth.

"I will learn ya dah dishwash'en business, boy," he promised me, finger pointing straight at my face for a bit of drama. "You gon-nah be dah best dishwash assistant," he informed me with great sincerity and pride.

I picked up the simple tasks quickly and he was very proud of the way we worked together as a team. Looking for brownie points, he told the boss that I was a smart kid and would go far.

My first responsibility was to scrape the left-over food off the plates and bowls and deposit them into the dishwasher racks. Then I'd slide the rack across the wet, soapy stainless-steel counter toward him and he would grab a long silver hose with a wide showerhead suspended from above and aim at each dish. The pulsating steamy hot water would quickly jettison the remaining loose food from the dishes.

Our uniform was a full-length, dark brown rubber apron intended to keep us dry; but the heat in the kitchen and the build-up of our perspiration had nowhere to go, so by two in the afternoon, we were drenched, our sneakers soaked and squishy.

We were a team. Freddy would pull up and open the dishwasher doors and, after the initial steaming, I would push the rack of dirty dishes in, as he pulled the steamy clean dishes out the other side and off to a drying station. He would then pull down the stainless-steel doors and push the greasy green 'start' button. The machine was old and the sound deafening, but it did clean the dishes well.

After a few days, he started to trust me to run the dishwasher on my own. After a few weeks, I noticed that Freddy was having trouble keeping up with me and was taking more and more cigarette breaks, telling me, "Take over, kid." One day he failed to show up for work and didn't call in; no one knew what happened, but he did show up the next day. It was clear that he had been drinking before he came to work. The boss smelled the alcohol and sent him home; he told him to come in sober the next day or he was out of a job. I never saw Freddy again.

I had other duties at the restaurant and they included bussing the tables, sweeping up, collecting the tips for the waitresses, and taking the trash out to the dumpster. To my surprise, at the end of my first day, the scrawny fortyish blond waitress handed me a fistful of crumpled bills, thinking that I would understand. I was so surprised, that I asked at once, "Why are you giving me this?"

She smiled and explained that I was a big help to the wait staff and that they all appreciated my being there to help out bussing; it made their job much easier and they wanted to share some of their tips with me. I was ecstatic, getting this windfall of unexpected cash.

Another colored man was hired through the local Manpower agency to take Freddy's place. I remember thinking about the Manpower agency that I passed a few times while driving with my father through a poor part of town. It made me think of slave auctions that I read about from the past. Only black men and women hanging around inside and out, smoking, drinking coffee, and waiting for a chance to serve white people.

The new man was not very friendly, kept to himself and worked very slow; he lasted only a few days. The boss asked if I could handle the dishwashing by myself for the last weeks of the summer before I returned to school, and I welcomed the opportunity. He gave me some extra cash on the side, but in hindsight, I suspect my mother had something to do with his generosity. So, in addition to doing the dishes without help, I continued to bus the tables and multitask.

Since I now had so many responsibilities, I worked out a system of periodically running between my different jobs. Of course, by the end of the day, I was totally exhausted, slept well, and was ready the next morning to get back to my job.

For me, the most anticipated event of each day was the lunch break. This was around two after the lunch crowd had dwindled. By then I was usually starving, and my legs were growing weak from all the standing and running about. It was a welcome break taking off the rubber apron and getting out of the sweltering kitchen. I sat at the end of the counter and most days ordered a hot roast beef sandwich with a pool of brown gravy in the middle of the mashed potatoes. The waitress behind the counter had taken a liking to me and gave me extra meat and gravy. I loved the gravy-soaked bread and washed it all down with a cherry coke.

I was quickly back at the dishwasher, with piles of grey plastic containers filled with dirty dishes waiting for my expert attention.

"Freddy would be proud," I thought as I pushed the loaded tray into the dishwasher and pressed the green button.

THE OLD BOYS' NETWORK

Bleary-eyed from lack of sleep, having been up most of the night with his newborn son, Frank rushes through the factory parking lot making a mental note to pick up the diapers and formula before heading home. Sara is stuck in the house with the flu and the baby.

Frank is dreading the sales meeting this morning because his performance has been on a downward spiral through the year and he's been frustrated by not being able to affect a change of direction and bring in new accounts. He ponders, "How long can I use the bad economy as an excuse?"

Willie's head throbs with each step from a severe migraine brought on by last night's bout of drinking with the boys and getting only three hours' sleep. He figures he will just 'coast' through the day and try to sneak out early.

Business in this company has been declining for several years and, this year, they will lose millions in revenue, because their competition has introduced a new affordable cost-savings product while they are still selling the same old equipment. Willie thinks, "It's hard to get an appointment with a potential or current account if I've got nothing new to offer but a free lunch for the buyer."

With briefcases in hand, laptops - loaded with less-than-factual bullshit sales projections - swung over their shoulders they walk quickly toward the building entrance and the eight o'clock weekly sales meeting.

Betty, the over-the-hill receptionist, her blue hair thinning by the year, greets one and all with her standard "Good morning! Have a lovely day!" in her screechy voice.

Willie cringes as he passes thinking, "It's bad enough when I don't have a migraine."

Jerry, his shoulders drooping, eyes on the ground, follows the sparkling grout lines between the highly buffed marble squares toward his office. For the tenth time this year, he's seriously thinking about looking for another job with better prospects. He sees the writing on the wall. His commissions have dwindled because of the lack of new sales and he's feeling the pinch, trying to make ends meet at home.

Then there's Mike, who is fifty-five today. Whenever he intends to persuade others of his point of view - which is often, and he's usually wrong - he invokes his self-proclaimed badge of credibility and, like a gorilla stomping his chest, proclaims, "I've worked here twenty-seven years and I can tell you this…"

Mr. Gilderstrom, the big cheese, is in from Duluth – unannounced. Not a good sign. The news travels like lightning and, within ten minutes, all 372 employees know that if the big boss is here unannounced, this cannot be a good-news day.

A general meeting of all department heads overrides all planned meetings and scheduled conference calls. The meeting lasts all of fifteen minutes and twelve white-as-sheep managers, sentenced to unemployment and financial stress, take the very long and lonely walk back to their charges to tell them that there will not be an 18th year for Sam nor a 28th year for Mike - or even another day for anyone. It's over. Today.

Jerry, in desperation, will be looking for another job with or without a future, because he lives from paycheck to paycheck with almost no savings. Frank will be agonizing how he will support his family and afford the condo apartment they recently purchased with a whopper of a mortgage.

And Gloria, a technician with two years' employment with the firm and her first job out of trade school, may soon be waiting tables in this already dying American industrial town; unless she takes the dive and relocates quickly and prays that all the technician jobs in her specialty have not been filled by workers in China or India, where people are happy to work a full six-day week for less than Gloria makes in a day.

With great sadness, Gloria returns her month-old sports car to the dealer because she can't make the payments, gives up her lovely apartment and moves back in with her parents. A month later, when all her prospects have run dry, she's back at her high-school job, waiting tables at the local diner.

What happened? Complacency by management. They thought their customers would buy from them forever. After all, they wined and dined them as often as possible.

What they failed to see was that, in the 21st century, the old boys' network is dead.

LITTLE GIRLS, PAST AND PRESENT

I now look at all little girls of two with new eyes and a far different perspective, as I experience the joys of visiting with my first granddaughter. One day, I visit and see her grappling with balance, weighing every step with caution, and just a few weeks later she's fearlessly flying across the room with lightning speed and confidence.

I think about my own daughter's first steps forty-five years ago, when I witnessed her delight to be off her knees and confident on her feet - to run - to play - to explore and experience her new freedom.

But this grandchild experience... because I see her through the eyes of a person who has already lived a full life, with more past than future, I must admit, she simply *takes my breath away*. Being with her and her little brother, seeing them do something unexceptional for the first time, is *exceptional* to me.

Besides Skype and FaceTime, I can replay the hundreds of accumulated photos and videos on my smartphone and relive days past and, as a doting grandparent, share them - sometimes even with strangers. Some pictures are almost identical with subtle differences in expression, but it's impossible for me to erase any of them because this would be akin to discarding wrinkled or torn hundred dollar bills.

My granddaughter has a wonderful and happy disposition, and I'm sure her parents have played an important role to this end. Her mother is a high-spirited, happy, positive, giving and committed person, so completely enjoying motherhood that it rubs off on both children. It's a joy to watch them together; they all adore and nurture each other.

I now go back to a very different and difficult time in my son's and daughter's family history. I go back 75 years to the city of Thessaloniki, Greece; a city where Sephardic Jews - cast out of Spain during the Inquisition - were welcomed by the occupying Ottoman Empire (Turks). For centuries, they made their home in this picturesque city on the Aegean. Before the Second World War, Jews outnumbered the Greek Orthodox Christians in the city, yet lived peacefully shoulder to shoulder with them.

From the 1600s, Sephardic Jews became a part of the fabric, the culture, and the economy of Thessaloniki and, along with the native Greek population, endured the bitter occupation of the Ottoman Empire. In spite of this occupation, together they built a fine city where international commerce, culture, Christian and Jewish traditions and personal life flourished. Until the German occupation, Thessaloniki was known as the 'Jerusalem of the Balkans'.

Theodore, my father-in-law, was then married to his first wife and they had a daughter. Hitler's henchmen came to this peaceful city, rounded up all the Jews and transported them to the rail yards, where they were stuffed mercilessly into cattle cars for the journey north. Most that survived this brutally inhumane trip were murdered - shot point blank when they got off the trains in Poland. Theodore's wife and daughter, as well as his brother, did not survive, but Theodore - an extremely resilient and resourceful man - lived to tell it all and start a new life.

After the camps were liberated, Theodore returned to Thessaloniki to find a dismal, destitute and broken city, void of family and friends or any way to make a living. He picked up the remaining pieces of his life, moved to Athens, courted and married a Jewish woman who had been hiding in the mountains with a Christian family during the war. They began their lives together in Athens, determined to leave Theodore's tragic past behind.

Theodore was a shrewd man and he started a business in Athens, buying, selling and trading all sorts of war surplus. When this merchandise started to dwindle, Theodore - having saved some money - made some connections in the United States. He came to New York with the hopes of importing bed sheeting, something badly needed and almost nonexistent in Greece through the war years. Theodore's business grew and he purchased a retail space in the Athens Agora, the marketplace below the Acropolis. His daughter and granddaughter (my daughter) now sell fashionable textiles at this same location.

Theodore and Stella bore two daughters. They bought an apartment in a nice, tree-lined residential neighborhood in Athens and sent their girls to the best private schools. When the older one started dating Christian boys (young Jewish men were almost non-existent then), he packed her off to the United States to stay with relatives in the hopes of her finding a Jewish husband, and... this is where I enter the picture.

Theodore's dream came true! He and Stella married their oldest daughter to a 'nice Jewish-American boy' - me! An unforgettable and legendary celebration followed in the Sephardic Temple on Long Island, where the band mingled traditional Greek dance music, Eastern European Jewish music, and popular rock n roll music. It was an event that all who attended - and that are still with us - remember fondly as one of the greatest weddings of their lives.

There was even more joy for Theodore and Stella when their daughter announced she was with child.

Theodore loved America. For him, it represented a country of amazing wealth and a place with a future for his daughter - and perhaps even his whole family. He knew that, if not for America, he would have likely not survived the war and the whole world would have quickly spiraled down to a cruel and evil place - much like it was in all of Europe and Asia during the war years.

He traveled to America often and always arrived with a suitcase full of juicy Greek tomatoes, tins of olive oil, and packages of chamomile tea. Theodore came to do business, he came to see his daughter, he came to walk the streets of Manhattan, to window-shop and enjoy the cheap steaks at Tad's Steakhouse. When his granddaughter was about to be born, he and not his Stella came for this big event and it was he that accompanied my wife and I, in the middle of the night, to the hospital.

From the time my daughter was born, it was clear that his priority was to spend as much time with her as possible. He came to America more often and his suitcase flowed with dainty little dresses and booties. There was no longer room for tomatoes and olive oil.

When I am with my granddaughter, I often think of Theodore's joy with my daughter. It was, without a doubt, the happiest period of his life. He was not a very sociable man, preferring to be with family and a few close friends, and I believe that either his tragic experiences and losses made him this way or perhaps it was his strong character that kept him steadfast through the worst that humanity could throw at him.

When he married Stella, they chose to leave the history of his previous marriage and child behind, and for 21 years never spoke a word of it to their daughters. It was only when a childhood friend of Stella's living near us in Queens - a Holocaust survivor from Greece - innocently spoke to my wife about Theodore's first wife and child, that the long-kept secret was revealed.

So now, when I am with my granddaughter, I sometimes think of Theodore and what he endured - beyond anything that I, growing up in the safety and security of America, could imagine. And I think of my little girl, 45 years ago, sitting on her grandfather's lap as both laughed and played together, manifesting his supreme joy *just to be with her* and to be 'in the moment' in her young life.

Theodore had a bad run of luck, having been placed in the path of a maniac and a society that had lost its moral compass, its social conscience, and its humanity. Even though he survived the wrath of the Third Reich, years later that evil society was responsible for cutting his life short with the Crohn's disease that he acquired from the unsanitary conditions and lack of nutritious food while in the concentration camps.

I am very lucky, very blessed to have been born in America, and I do not for a moment take for granted my father-in-law's journey, his unimaginable loss, his personal suffering and struggle for survival. I know beyond a doubt that, if he had not been incredibly strong, resolute and determined to survive, my wife would never have been, my daughter would never have been, my son would never have been, and my beautiful granddaughter *would never have been.*

HOME IN THE BECKET WOODS

For millennia, it was a forest. Then, in the early seventeenth century, it became a farm for early settlers escaping European tyrants. After a few generations, it became a forest again, because there were now far better places to farm, where the land was richer, flat, with less clay and fewer rocks vibrating their way to the surface.

Each time I visited my son at his summer camp in this wooded mountain hamlet, I realized that a special calm and tranquility would come over me, resonating in some 'out-of-body fashion' as if I had been here in a prior life. So, I borrowed some money from my dad and purchased a few acres, hoping to one day place a small house on the land as a summer retreat. Perhaps it could be a wonderful place to grow old with nature.

One fall weekend, after purchasing the land, my daughter and I came to the woods from our high-rise apartment in Manhattan. We chopped down some small trees and created a narrow path to nowhere through the two acres of heaven that was teeming with life. We cut the trees into eighteen inch logs and stacked them neatly into a pyramid shape near the front of the property to announce to the world that someone had claimed this piece of paradise. We put up POSTED signs because that what 'city people' do when they buy property in the woods for the first time.

Little by little, an area was cleared for a small foundation and a small log house was built in the summer, fall and early winter of 1987. It was all of 800 square feet and built from a popular Lincoln Log kit, delivered on one flatbed truck. It contained thick logs for the exterior walls, plywood floors, and unfinished 2x4 interior framing.

My father came on weekends and wired the house, reviving his skills from his WWII shipyard days. Along with Alfredo - my father's friend and retired cabinet maker - they installed the basic kitchen I had purchased from Home Depot. I also bought some wide ponderosa pine boards, allowed them to dry out for several months and, with the help of a friend, we installed the floor. Today, many years later, it's one of the special features of this house, giving it a homey, warm look and feel that hardwoods cannot achieve.

Little by little, we added tongue-and-groove pine interior walls, creating bedroom, den and bathroom spaces. We installed very basic kitchen and bathroom fixtures, being on a tight budget back then.

For the first five years, weeds grew wild and high around the house and, every so often, I'd make an attempt to cut them down with a weed-whacker; but they grew fast in the woods and, within a week, they were knee-high again. From early spring, the weeds teemed with bugs and field mice and with the sounds of crickets, bees and hornets. We had invaded their space and the insects and mice invited themselves into our house, letting us know that we were on the land that they had occupied for centuries.

I stained the walls a wonderful honey color, bringing out the beauty and texture of the pine. I took time off from work while the scaffolding was still in place, so I could be a Michelangelo, on my back, staining the cathedral ceilings. In the spring and summer, I slowly started to plant some bushes, a Japanese maple - still standing through all the brutal winters - and I hired a local landscaper to build beautiful stone retaining walls, stairs and entry paths, and to plant grass and shrubs around the house. I built a terracotta stone hearth in the living room and added a wood-burning stove. In the first bathroom, I set down basic white tile and, when we built an addition, I added a beautiful slate floor. I learned as I worked. Those original floors are still with us.

After 'escaping' Manhattan and moving our business to the Berkshires, this became our only home. It was small and comfortable, but Karen and I knew that it would be necessary to enlarge it so that two people with varied interests would not be subjected to sharing such a small space.

After five years, we completed our office building in Lee, and our thoughts and priorities shifted to enlarging the house. We hired a builder. I acted as the contractor, relying on the local building inspector for advice, and to make sure the sub-contractors didn't take advantage with shoddy short-cuts or by using inferior materials. And the work began.

It took close to a year to build the addition and it took several more months to add an enclosed porch and decks all around the house. At the last minute, I decided to add a cupola for Karen so she could have her own private space to meditate and read, high above the bedroom with panoramic windows and skylights to spy the forest through the trees.

Little by little, the house was complemented with things of beauty and convenience that brought pleasure, peace, and happiness to our lives as we worked on the many challenges of building our business - sometimes wondering if it would survive.

After many years, we needed to replace the decks and add some amenities - like a massive covered entry over the front door, held up with 12" thick tree trunks. The small, cheap metal entry door that we had opened and closed thousands of times was replaced by an impressive stained-glass double door. When someone enters the house for the first time, they are usually overwhelmed by the space and the beautiful and harmonious decorations and artwork.

We also purchased two adjoining acres so no one could build a house on the land above us. It took time adjusting to living in the woods, but thirty years later, the last thing we want is neighbors with barking dogs and crying children to break the serenity of this sacred place.

The house is on a dirt road that we share with bear, deer, turkey, fox, porcupines and many species of birds. The winters are harsh, but we've learned how to pass them with minimum discomfort. When spring comes, we appreciate it far more than a city dweller could ever imagine.

The house was just stained again, a new boiler installed and the roof will need to be replaced soon. These projects will keep the house a home for many years to come. I come and go, but for Karen, this is her sanctuary and I know that every day she enjoys waking up here and every day she loves to return. I am very happy about this.

When you purchase a piece of forest, clear it, set a foundation, watch the log walls go up one level at a time, and you are intimate with every nail and every screw that has ever been hammered or screwed in, and have nurtured it as you would a child, it becomes part of you and leaving it for good would be as difficult as leaving a loved one for good. Indeed, the house has become a living and breathing entity to be nurtured, cared for, talked to, embraced and loved as you would a child.

And through the windows, skylights, and doors, you can see the trees and, through the trees, the living forest.

JUST WATCH ME!

Watchmakers spend generously on slick advertising to encourage sports enthusiasts to buy their timepieces. Their tacit claim: if you own one of our classic watches, you too may become an Olympic gold medalist, an MVP, a famous golf or tennis pro, the fastest sprinter, swimmer or race car driver on the planet, or a sailor on the winning America's Cup team. And even if you don't make it big, you buy into the snob appeal of being associated with life's sporting winners.

The harbinger of trust, time is the one element that cannot be disputed. Some classic watch brands have been around for generations and promote themselves as symbols of personal and professional excellence. They sponsor major sports events and use nostalgia to claim their place in the history of a sport. They have kept some sports alive and fostered comradery between teams, players and enthusiasts.

Putting common sense aside, I move past the obvious: that watch manufacturers are simply selling watches with the help of famous athletes' endorsements. We all know that athletes who endorse a brand do so for the money. I decide that there is a quiet mythology behind all this, one that resonates *success for all of us*. Success to reach our impossible dream, which - maybe - is not so impossible after all.

I've never paid much attention to glitzy watch windows or store displays. When in a large department store, I'm usually on my way to a clothing sale on the men's floor. But now that I'm curious, I decide to fantasize about investing in a serious, expensive timepiece for myself.

I'm discovering a watch culture of both silly and convincing claims authored and conceived by hungry sales folk. One young man quietly tells me, "Tiger Woods was given his first blah-blah by his father and he's worn one ever since."

"Who knows if it's true," I think, but it's part of the big picture and something to ponder. I'm overwhelmed with the profusion of style, color, and materials. Some have diamond faces, some sport clusters of tiny hands and barely readable numbers, and some have questionable and elusive 'never-to-be-used-by-most' features.

There are so many inspiring ads with world-renowned and accomplished athletes promoting these little tickers, that I feel I must cast common sense aside and believe on some level in a connection between the timepiece and our sports hero's personal success. 'Play the role - believe it - and become it', as motivational speakers often preach.

Behind each glass counter display, a sales associate is dressed in concert with the image of the brand. The more expensive the brand, the better dressed the sales associate.

After spending hours navigating what I've coined *'watch-scape'* and methodically selecting some likely candidates - making notes, considering and seeking out the most inspiring watches hopefully within my price range - I find myself holding one that makes my heart race. Holding my breath, I flip the tag to see if it's within my budget. It isn't and represents six weeks' take-home pay.

Acting on pure impulse and adrenaline, I hear the words

"I'll take it" come from my lips. Did I say that? I did. Since I've come this far I've decided to throw logic, sensibility, my life-long frugality and family values to the wind.

"I've taken the plunge," I tell myself. "It's a once-in-a-lifetime indulgence and, possibly, if those inspirational watch campaigns have a shred of truth in them, I may elevate my game by my commitment to the purchase of this timepiece. It will be my muse, my confidante, my partner. I too will experience the joyous moment of the win, the kill, the hole-in-one and maybe even a chance at a world-class victory.

I fumble through my wallet for the plastic and feel its resistance to emerge, knowing that it will create serious debt for me. I quickly flip it to the salesperson who, with equal speed and aplomb, swipes and hands it back to me with the paper stub and a pen for my John Hancock. Deal done, and we both experience a sigh of relief and closure. I have the watch and the sales associate can pay his rent, due last week.

I've always wanted to be a great golfer with a low handicap, to play on the best courses with the best players and - of course - win and win often. I'd love to have a reputation as 'a great golfer' so other players will seek me out to improve their game. I'd like an invite to the Masters, to be a player and observer on the world's major golf links, shoot the breeze with others aspiring to become professionals, and then - even if it's a pipe dream today - relive with the pros their finest moments. On my way up, they won't know me, but they *will* recognize the iconic watch I wear, and perhaps that will break the ice and be an incentive for them to chat with me.

After a year, my golf score improved dramatically and a golf buddy asked me to what I attributed my advancement? I tell him that I'm confident and I tell him about my watch and my success theory. I could see him laughing at me through his eyes, but he must question his skepticism because my game is now so much better than his.

Several months pass, my buddy has just returned from Shenzhen, China, where counterfeit 'street' watches are sold in every alley. On his wrist is an almost identical copy of my iconic watch. "I paid fifty bucks for this baby, probably overpaid!" he laughs, and with a big grin and a deep voice says, "Let's see what this baby will do for *my* game!"

"Yes," I say with a big smile on my face, "Let's see."

Years pass.

I have worked very hard at my game, inspired by my watch and the famous golfers endorsing and wearing it. I have made it to the pro circuit, my picture appears in print almost daily, and sports jocks scramble for a photo op and an interview. I also now promote my timepiece maker for a six-figure payday each year. I do it for the money, but - between you and me - I know that the watch did play a big role in my success. It's not clear how much I needed the expensive watch to inspire me and keep me on the track to success, but what I do know is that the day I dropped three grand for a watch, I made a personal commitment to myself and gave myself a gift: the chance to make my dreams come true.

I wear my watch almost every day. It's now an old friend. I let my little boy and girl try it on, even though it is far too big for them, but I know that they will grow into it. My old golfing buddy is still playing golf on the home course, his street watch stopped running long ago, and he's still struggling with his embarrassing handicap.

TRAM PEOPLE

I was looking out of my bathroom window, admiring my very first morning view from my new apartment overlooking the East River and the Ed Koch Queensboro Bridge. The Roosevelt Island tram suddenly slid surprisingly close to my window. I was startled and could clearly see the faces of the passengers for a few seconds as they sailed by. I thought, "If I can see them, can they see me?" It was of particular importance because I was naked and my first impulse was to drop the shade, which I did, even though it was likely too late.

After the first day, each morning, when my eyes were still half-glued shut, I looked forward to looking out of my bathroom 'window to the world'. Anticipating the tram's passing from Roosevelt Island to Manhattan became part of my daily routine, and it never failed to amuse and entertain me. I realized that, if I kept the lights off, I could see out and the tram people would probably not see me. I only had a few moments each day to scan the faces and clothing of the tram people. Because I was separated by glass and space, in a strange way I felt they were not *real people*, just actors in a movie that repeated each day with almost the same cast but wearing different clothing. I became more observant with each passing day and soon I knew the faces of most of the actors who passed by at 7:02, at 7:17, and (after my shower) at 7:32. I gave each of the regulars fictitious names – most inspired by their faces, demeanor, and clothing. Sometimes I spoke to them out loud, knowing they could not possibly hear me.

"Margaret," I scolded, "that shade of lipstick is terrible! It makes you look like a cheap hooker." "Jack, you have too many pens in your shirt pocket and you look like a super nerd. SUPER NERD, can you hear me?" And then, "Audrey, you look beautiful as ever. Each day you wear such stunning clothing. I'm kind of envious – where do you shop?" I named her after Audrey Hepburn because she was petite, wore her hair short, and dressed clean, classic and sophisticated. "Max, you little fart! You dumpy, little, scuzzy-looking man, I wonder what woman would want to share a bed with you? How come you only shave on Mondays?"

Sometimes, I wished I could capture the collective thoughts of the tram people for just a minute or two. I fantasized that the scope of their thoughts would range from the mundane "Did I turn the light out in the kitchen?" to the very interesting "I wish I could tell the IRS that my boss is cheating big time." And in some cases (from the most innocent-looking, prim and proper woman in a style-less dress) the quite shocking: "I think I'd enjoy making love with that tall young man over in the corner. Look at the size of his hands!"

My 'James', a very attractive dapper dresser in his mid-thirties, usually stared out of the glass doors in my direction, always appearing lost in thought. Maybe the tram ride helped him separate from reality and just chill for six minutes.

I became intrigued with my James. I gave him this name because I thought he looked like a well-dressed British butler with the sex appeal and bad boyish looks of James Dean. Each day, as I sauntered into the bathroom, I would play mind games and try to guess the color or design of his shirt and tie, the color of his suit - would he wear that chic royal blue blazer with the silver buttons today? He had lots of solid white, light blue and light pink shirts and a wide range of striped shirts as well. When he wore the solid shirts, he always wore a traditional Ivy League diagonally striped tie. You know, the kind you find at Brooks Brothers.

Monday's outfit was a given for my James. Without fail, he wore a dark navy suit, a white shirt, and a bright red tie. I figured this was his version of a Monday morning power outfit, possibly to mask his weekend hangover or impress his superiors, or both.

I was between relationships - free and available - and I felt comfortable fantasizing about meeting James one day and possibly having a romantic encounter, or even wedding bells and little ones after a few years of enjoying each other without interruption. I wondered at times if he had a girlfriend, was married, had kids – was possibly gay? It intrigued me, stimulated my imagination, and simultaneously stressed me out! I wanted to know all about my James and I felt powerless to know any more than my fantasy, just seeing him pass my window each weekday and wondering how he spent his weekends.

One night, I couldn't sleep and sat staring out of my living room window, listening to the dulled-down sounds of the city. It was 3 AM and the traffic on the bridge consisted of just a trickle of cabs, limos, delivery trucks, and an occasional ambulance, its flashing red lights invading my apartment, bouncing off my walls and mirrors.

"Who's coming to Manhattan at this ungodly hour?" I thought. "Late arrivals from the airport? Swing shift hospital workers? A couple rushing to a New York hospital to give birth? A baker heading to work? A one night stand?"

I fell asleep on the window sill. At dawn, I opened my

eyes slightly, to be greeted by slivers of sun dancing and glistening from the East River. At times, ominous whirlpools proclaimed "The tide is coming in!" as seawater rushed up and collided with the opposite flow of the East River, and the confluence of the Harlem River and the Long Island Sound.

It was 7:17 and I was about to put on my blouse over my white shelf bra when something stopped me. The bathroom light was on and I realized in that split second that the tram was about to pass. I decided I really wanted James to see me in my bra. I glanced in the mirror, smiled approvingly at my drop-dead cleavage, my sculpted shoulders and arms. "I am hot, man!" I thought. My unrealistic fantasy was that James would see me, find me, and sweep me off my feet.

"How crazy am I?" I mused, using my breasts like twin strobes, like a wiggling worm on a hook, like the bewitching singing of the sirens to Odysseus and his crew of horny men. I turned again to the mirror and said out loud, "If he's not blind or gay, he won't deny this cleavage. Years of working out have paid off," I thought, as I threw modesty to the window, hoping that only Mr. Perfect would see me and not the whole damn 7:17 tram crowd. I stood motionless, innocently looking down at the river and street below as if I was in deep thought and unaware of the passing tram.

When the tram was right in my cross-hairs, I looked up and quickly scanned the familiar faces, searching for my James. There he was, looking straight ahead for a change. At that moment, I didn't give a damn who saw me in or out of my bra, as long as *he* did. So, thumbs under my straps, I slipped my bra down completely. It was exhilarating! I couldn't believe that I was doing something so irrational and so not me! "Mom would not approve," I thought with a naughty little giggle. "And Dad, well he would be too embarrassed to say anything."

I slipped my bra back on when the tram passed by, my heart racing and totally confident that James saw me for those few seconds. While applying my lipstick, I thought about how I could connect with my dream guy. In addition to knowing what he looked like, I knew that on Mondays he would wear the same basic outfit. If I got up early and arrived at the tram station exit when the 7:18 and the 7:23 trams arrived, I was sure to spot him as he came down the stairs, but - what then? If he recognized me, maybe he would stop dead in his tracks and say something spontaneously like, "You look familiar. Do I know you?"

"It was a long shot but what the hell," I thought. If he did ask that question, I would retort with, "Perhaps you remember this?" and open up my jacket, cleavage on display.

The next Monday I had a bad hair day and a killer headache, and I realized that I was not on my best form to meet my James. I decided that I would do the bra/no bra exhibition one more time - just to make sure James saw me. I did and, to my great pleasure, in that five-second 'window', we connected. He looked my way and saw my half-naked body. His head jerked back in surprise and he looked around to see if anyone else saw what he did. No question about it, he saw me in the flesh - that was a given - and I was positive he would recognize me next Monday morning when I'd be at the tram to greet him.

On Monday, I dressed early in a classic Coco Chanel tight little black dress. I walked to the tram and, with great anticipation, waited for James to come down the stairs. He was not there for the first tram or the second and, in desperation, I waited for several more trams to arrive. I repeated the trip to the tram each day that week - but no James. I looked for him from my window each day for several weeks. It was official…he was gone.

A year and a half passed and it was Christmas Day. I left my apartment and entered the elevator - and you will never guess who was in the elevator! I was sure it was my long-lost and almost-forgotten James. Words fell out of my mouth: "Good morning!" followed by "Have you ever lived on Roosevelt Island?" He was wearing a blue suit, white shirt, and red tie. I was sure it was him.

"Yes," he said. "I lived there for a few years before getting married and then I moved for a while to Jersey, but unfortunately the marriage didn't work out."

He asked me how I knew, and I smiled and opened up my coat. I was wearing a deep-plunge red dress and he looked down at my cleavage and smiled. He said, "You're the woman in the window, the one I passed each day on the tram, aren't you?" He went on, "I've thought about you often, fantasizing that maybe your little performance may have been for my benefit, you know – like a tease?"

As the doors opened, I responded with my most inviting smile and the sexiest voice I could muster, "You are correct. It *was* for you and now I've found you!*"*

His real name? Johnny. Close enough!

REALITY ONE, REALITY TWO

It comes when least expected.
It sneaks up, overwhelms;
When consumed by it,
There can be no fight.

In a parallel reality...
It feels so, so good.
True love is a best friend,
A prized, but vulnerable asset.

In Reality One, it cannot be shaken
Without great pain and anguish.
In Reality Two, one cannot be convinced
That it is gone, when it seems still so alive.

Helpless am I in its grip; I wonder
Is it equally gripping you?
An energy and spirit of its own,
Buzzing always in the head.

I cannot touch it, even when it touches me.
I cannot quantify it, it has no borders.
I cannot qualify it as anything because
That emotion has yet to be born on earth.

It's with us from wake up
'Til the moment of slumber.
It finds us in dreams,
Pleasant or bitter.

At will, we can leave Reality Two, pass back
To Reality One, and recall any day, any moment,
Any embrace, smile and pleasure.
Reality One - my choice.

SWIM TUBE

Remember when you were very small and you waited with great anticipation as your father huffed and puffed, struggling to blow up your first swimming tube?

Remember the feel of the plastic under your arms, the smell, and the colorful pictures of turtles, fish, seashells, and seahorses?

Remember splashing into the water with your tube for the very first time? Remember when suddenly there was no ground under your feet, and you were being held up by air, floating?

Remember bouncing lightly above the water as you and the other children exuberantly splashed and laughed - and your parents watched close by, waiting for you to feel safe and secure in your tube?

Remember becoming independent of the tube and swimming on your own? Remember the feeling of being independent and no longer needing a tube of air to sustain you?

Remember becoming an adult, no longer protected each day by your parents, and being totally responsible for your needs?

When you discard the *swim tube of parental protection* and swim solo in the deep water of life, you join adulthood.

Not before, no matter how old you are.

THE HEARTLESS DIAL TONE

For the first time in years, Freddy climbs the rickety, drop-down ladder to his attic. His goal is to find a family portrait his sister has asked him for. While searching, he comes across his dusty high school yearbook and cracks it open, dust billowing in his eyes. He slowly closes it. He doesn't find the portrait for his sister and decides to bring the yearbook down instead.

"Memories of youth," he muses, as he robotically reaches into the bag of popcorn, craving the next spike of salt, stuffing handfuls in his mouth. With his other hand, he flips the pages of the yearbook, barely listening to the drone of the monosyllabic ten o'clock news reporter who has nothing important to say.

He remembers the night of the senior prom, watching his high school sweetheart laughing, hand-in-hand with Richie - his best friend - as they disappear off the edge of the ball field into the dark woods. It was a huge betrayal by both his steady girl and best pal, but mostly, by his lifelong friend. The emotions of that night - long forgotten - return. After the prom, he successfully blocked both Sarah and Richie from his thoughts and never saw or spoke to either of them again.

He hadn't thought about Sarah at all until he came across her picture in the yearbook. Now he recalls her sexy voice, beautiful hazel eyes, pointed nose, thin lips, and short-cropped, frizzy red hair. He thinks back to their first awkward and passionate kiss, and this - coalescing with memories of the carefree summer days spent fishing and catching frogs with Richie - creates a bittersweet and uncomfortable moment for him.

Freddy prepares to leave the couch and head to bed. He stretches his legs, rotates his feet left and right, and slowly rotates his head, hearing the tiny neck bones crackling in his ears. It is ten thirty and he hasn't heard a word of the evening news. He clicks off the T.V. and tosses the empty popcorn bag into the wood-burning stove; he turns the damper down, grabs the wobbly handrail and methodically - one step at a time - pulls his heavy body up the threadbare, soiled, carpeted stairs.

After a restless night, Freddy wakes up depressed and lethargic, lacking the ambition to push the covers from his warm body, unwilling to meet the frosty morning air. "I am alone," he thinks, in his self-induced melancholy. But this is an old story; his self-pity getting the upper hand. "I need to get into the shower," he mumbles under his breath and struggles out of bed, anticipating the hot water pounding on his head and neck, knowing this will prepare him to meet the day and then, hopefully, *things will return to normal*. He shuffles into the bathroom and is momentarily startled by what he 'thinks' he sees in the mirror out of the corner of his eye. "I must be losing my mind," he thinks, his eyes not yet fully open. He dismisses the image and turns on the shower.

Now fully awake, and in a much more positive mood, he returns to the sink and runs a towel over the fogged mirror. He is shocked by what he sees: the Freddy of his youth looking back at him. "I must still be in bed dreaming," he thinks, as the blood rushes to his head, his heart pounding, feeling faint. Disoriented, he grabbed the edges of the sink, leans forward to take a closer look at his young man's face in the mirror. He splashes cold water on it, hoping that *things would return to normal*. "Did I die in my sleep?" he thinks.

At that very moment, the phone rings. He turns away from the mirror and stares at the phone on the table just outside the bathroom door. He considers that, if he answers it, he will know for sure if this is all just a bad dream.

"Who is it?" he inquires and a faint, barely audible voice of a young woman, sounding like a scratchy old record responds, "Is this Freddy?"

"Yes, it's Freddy, who are you?" Freddy asks anxiously.

"This is Sarah. We went to high school together... we dated as seniors." Guarded and tentative, she asks if he remembers her, even though he knows she knows he will remember that night of her youthful, heartless betrayal.

"Sarah, is it really you?" Freddy asks, again feeling faint as he waits for her answer. After a good ten seconds, he hears … 'click' and she's gone and the heartless dial tone returns.

For the next few days, he works late to keep his mind off the strange happenings that have shaken his world and brought back bitter memories. When he arrives home, he bypasses the living room and ten o'clock news and drags himself straight up the stairs. He brushes his teeth, sets his alarm, and is out as soon as his head hits the pillow - exactly the way he has planned it.

When he wakes on Saturday morning, before he even opens his eyes, he finds himself thinking of a toasted sesame bagel laden with cream cheese, onions, capers, and smoked salmon. He is now highly motivated. Forgetting about Sarah and Richie, he jumps out of bed and heads for the shower. He trips over his yearbook and - momentarily forgetting about the shower - picks up the book and sits on the edge of the bed, trying to decipher some of the scribbled comments and names long forgotten. He looks again at Sarah's picture and also at his 'good friend'. He decides to take the book with him to The Bagel Nook, thinking it will entertain him during breakfast.

The bagel is so, so good, and he orders a second and refills his coffee cup three times. He knows his pants are already too tight, but after that scare in the mirror on Tuesday, and the weird phone call, he rationalizes the second bagel. He thinks to himself, "Basically, Richie was a good kid and I shouldn't hold a grudge at his adolescent behavior so long ago." He continues thinking, as he focuses on their photos: "After all, we were just kids back then, and our values and personalities were just developing and evolving." He decides then that, if he ever bumps into them, he will act civil and wouldn't show any signs of resentment.

He notices that the age marks on his hands are fading. "Strange," he thinks, as he navigates the second bagel; and each time he picks up the bagel or coffee, the age marks became noticeably lighter.

His plan, when the food is gone, is to shop for some socks and underwear. He closes the yearbook, stretches, stands up and, to his embarrassment, his pants fall down, exposing his underwear; he catches them at the hip. He looks around to see if anyone witnessed the event, hears a giggle, and he quickly pulls them up, tightening the belt to the very last hole (never used before); but the pants are still loose. He is in a panic because he realizes that something crazy is happening again, and this horrifies him because it confirms that the first incident with the mirror and the phone call *really did happen.*

Holding his paper cup in one hand and the yearbook in the other, he pushes on the exit door with his shoulder but doesn't notice that someone is, at that moment, pulling it open from the outside. He goes flying through the door into the street and nearly loses his balance, managing to avoid spilling his coffee. A young man catches him, preventing what would have been a nasty collision with two women, the younger pushing a baby carriage.

He apologizes to the women and turns to thank the young man. As he focuses on the young man's face, terror strikes and he thinks his heart will stop as he realizes that it is Richie - who he was looking at in his yearbook just moments earlier - the one that betrayed him in his youth

"Richie?" Freddy inquires.

"Freddy?" Richie inquires.

In this time-warp moment, each sees the other as they were many years earlier.

"Funny we should bump into each other here because I was just going through our high school yearbook," says Freddy, as he holds it up, "and I was looking at your and Sarah's pictures. It's strange, but I've had weird thoughts about both of you for weeks."

"Me too!" Richie blurts out. "How weird!" he continues with some consternation in his voice.

Sarah, the young woman with the baby carriage, stares at her two schoolmates in incredulous disbelief. It was their voices that first got her attention and when she looked up, she confirmed it really was them. She had also recently looked at her high school yearbook and also received a strange call one morning from Freddy and another from Richie - and each had hung up after a few moments.

She comes over and they all hug. Sarah tells the boys that, one morning, she saw herself in the bathroom mirror as a teenager, without the wrinkles, without the sagging jowls, sporting her teen bangs. (She leaves out the part where her boobs are back up where they were during her youth.)

Three adults, having thought of each other at *precisely the same moment in time* - remembering each other as they were in their youth - have wandered into the little-known, oft-whispered-about (by mystics and relativity theorists) 'reality-free time warp' that exists on the fringes of time, space, and relativity.

Freddy, Richie, and Sarah never share their experiences of having visited their black hole - their personal corner of the human puzzle.

Why *would* they share?

No one would believe them.

THE SAILBOAT AND THE MOTORBOAT

When you arrive at your job each day, you come as a sailboat or as a motorboat. The water represents your job and the vessel represents who you are.

As a motorboat: You arrive and start the engine, check the fuel gauge, push the throttle, and zoom across the water to your destination. Your hull barely touches or experiences the water at all; it barely senses the temperature, waves, wind, and tide. At the end of the day, you zoom back to your slip, turn off the ignition, and you are gone till your next adventure.

As a sailboat: You check the direction and speed of the wind, the tide, the sails, and the rigging. You check the auxiliary outboard, the weather report, and you observe the size of the waves and speed of the wind. You cautiously make your way to the open sea, always checking the luff of your sail, the tug on your sheets, and the position of your boom. Deep in the water, the rudder, keel and hull report back what the boat is experiencing as you glide through the waves. At the end of the day, you return to your slip and run down your mental checklist of what must be done to secure your boat for the night - and possibly your next day of sailing.

The motorboat represents those of you who *do not* own your job. You skim over your work throughout the day, barely touching or thinking about anything more than necessary, producing only what is minimally required of you. At the end of the day, you shut off your computer, grab your keys, and leave the workplace. You rush out the door and don't think about your job again until the next morning, when you turn on your computer and - like yesterday and every day - you skim across your job, watching the clock for break-time, lunch-time, and quit-time. When the clock strikes five, you are history till tomorrow.

The sailboat represents those of you who *own* your job. From dawn till dusk, before, during, and after your work hours, you are involved. You consider everything important and you diligently work toward greater efficiency and success for the business, earning your pay every day. You sometimes skip the breaks, take shorter lunches, and stay late if there are deadlines. At day's end, you leave your work area neat, possibly with a 'To Do' list that will greet you the next morning. It's likely that, if there were challenges or problems during the day, you think about how to resolve the problem on the way home and over breakfast. When you arrive at your work area the next day, you hit the ground running, already knowing many of your goals for the day.

So, are you a motorboat or a sailboat?

THE GIFT OF CLOSURE

Fast forward forty-three years. It's now 2005 and I am again about to depart for Johannesburg, South Africa from JFK International Airport - this time on a Jet and, this time, a direct flight.

My hair is mostly grey now, my waist has gone from 32 to 36, and I leave America today with wrinkles and a much different outlook on life than before. I'm anxious to see the 'new South Africa', orchestrated by Nelson Mandela and the African National Congress.

When I was twenty-one, a young woman of twenty came to the U.S. from South Africa with her father, who was the representative of the textile company I worked for in New York City. It was the spring of 1961 and, my being the only single man in the office, her father asked if I would take his daughter Yvette out and 'show her around town'. I agreed. She liked me, I liked her - we hit it off at once and she told her father she wanted to stay in New York longer. Through a political connection of her father's, she was able to secure a job at the United Nations, and this allowed her to stay for as long as she had the job. We spent a glorious year dating; my picking her up most weekends on the Upper East Side of Manhattan, where she stayed with distant cousins of her father.

It was now a few months after the assassination of John F. Kennedy. I departed from what was then New York's Idlewild Airport (now JFK) with a one-way ticket to Johannesburg, South Africa. I was traveling bottom-of-the-barrel economy. The first leg of the trip was via Icelandic Airways and, then, with South African TREK airways for the remainder of the trip across three continents. The first leg of the trip was to Reykjavik on a four-engine prop. After a short fuel stop at Reykjavik, we flew through the night and the next morning arrived in Luxembourg. Some five hours later, we boarded an old German plane chartered by Trek Airways for a short hop over to London. During the layover at Gatwick, I located the Western Union kiosk and sent my South African girlfriend a telegram announcing, "I am coming to South Africa and the reason I didn't let you know sooner was because I didn't want to be talked out of coming. I will be on the Trek Airways flight landing in Jo'burg at 11 AM on Tuesday." I sent it with my heart in my mouth, literally.

That trip was a young man's desperate attempt to put a love affair with a lovely Jewish girl from Johannesburg back on track. We had fallen in love during her year-long visit to New York and had what I believed to be a match made in heaven, one I was sure would last a lifetime. After a year in the U.S., she needed to leave for a while to represent her family at a bar mitzvah in London, and then she would go back to South Africa for the summer; she planned to return to the U.S. in the fall. Understandably, her parents had different feelings and did not want to lose their daughter to infrequent and short visits halfway across the planet - so they refused to fund her trip back.

I read her 'Dear John' letter again and again. I couldn't believe it, I was heartbroken, devastated, and out of my mind with disappointment. In hindsight, reading between the lines now, I don't think she was totally convinced she *should* return to the U.S., a place where she had no roots and only two aged and distant relatives. In any case, I had to go to South Africa and was able to scrape up the cost of a one-way ticket. My insane intention was to marry her and live in South Africa.

Because of apartheid, South African planes were banned from much of African airspace, and the fact that the plane was a prop - with less than half the speed and range of a jet - meant the trip took another two days. We traveled *between* the Italian Alps because the plane was not pressurized and couldn't fly over the mountains; the scenery was spectacular. We had a wonderful view of the Straits and Rock of Gibraltar, the Amalfi coast, and much of the beautiful Italian coastline.

Because the plane flew low, mostly 3,000 to 5,000 feet above sea level, every important landmark was visible to the naked eye, something that is all but impossible these days, unless you are on a small private plane. In hindsight, it was an adventure of a lifetime.

We first landed for fuel in the Canary Islands; then again in Lagos, Nigeria; then onto Brazzaville, The Congo. We had gone to sleep with the sun setting on one side of the plane as we flew about 2,000 feet over the Sahara Desert, and woke the next morning - still over the Sahara - with the sun rising on the opposite side of the plane.

When we touched down at Brazzaville's airport, several short and very black men boarded the plane, their skin shining from the humidity, as they proceeded to spray the cabin and passengers with a horrible-smelling bug killer. Everyone gagged, coughed, and rubbed their eyes and, after a few minutes, we were allowed to deplane, breath in the fresh air, and stretch out on the tarmac in the intense and very humid 100-degree plus Equatorial heat. The jungle framed the airport on all sides with brilliant shades of green and that first sweet smell of Africa still remains vivid in my nostrils and memory.

"Africa! Africa!" I thought again and again during the twenty minutes on the tarmac in the blistering heat. "Africa! It's so raw, so untamed, so primitive, and so beautiful."

Surreal and magical sounds were coming from the jungle: the varied screeching of birds and monkeys, and I think I heard a few lions communicating. It was a wonderful, out-of-body experience for me. I believe to this day that, at that moment, I acquired the wanderlust that has taken me around the globe through my life - and my bucket list keeps growing.

After short fuel stops in Luanda, Angola and then Bulawayo, Southern Rhodesia, the plane finally touched down and taxied to the terminal at Jan Smuts International Airport in Johannesburg.

I remember the butterflies in my stomach and thought, "Would Fritz, Yvette's father, be so angry that I came - uninvited and expecting to stay at his home - that he would have the authorities turn me around for the next flight home? I came down the steps onto the tarmac, walked slowly toward the arrivals building, squinting in the bright sunlight and looking for that beautiful face and short curly hair that I missed like crazy. To my great joy and relief, I saw Yvette and her dad. They had seen me first and were already waving with big smiles. I was overwhelmed with relief and gratitude for their open-arm welcome. What a relief! I had not been turned back.

At the airport, I was faced for the first time with the ugly face of apartheid. It took me completely by surprise and made me feel disoriented and numb with disbelief. Water fountains and bathrooms that we take for granted were marked 'whites only' and 'blacks'. For starters, I couldn't comprehend why there was a need for separate water fountains. Even though I knew about apartheid from a distance, when faced with it, I realized that I was mentally, emotionally, and culturally unprepared for this cruel repression of the majority of the population - even though there were places in America that were still not much better.

When Yvette was in the States, we went to Jones Beach and she told me it was the first time in her life that she saw black people in bathing suits. By the end of her year in America, in spite of her highly prejudiced upbringing, she had made some black friends at her job. After all, the United Nations was culturally diverse and it was a given that that would happen. I attended the *bon voyage* party her office friends made for her when she left, where she tearfully hugged and kissed her new black friends - an emotional first for her since this was a serious crime at that time in South Africa.

In Johannesburg, many white families had televisions that they had imported from Germany in anticipation of having entertainment that the rest of the civilized world was already enjoying. A sleek transmission tower was built in Johannesburg, but it would not be used for many, many years for anything other than an observation tower.

So the expensive, imported televisions gathered dust as the government grappled with their concerns over security. Afrikaners (white descendants of Dutch settlers) - the most radical of South African whites and the group running the government- contended that television would be too risky because if there was a revolt, the stations would be the first place the black revolutionists would go to incite and unite the repressed native population. They also hyped the theory that male servants watching television in white folk's homes - and seeing scantily dressed white women - would get excited and be encouraged to rape their master's wives and daughters. Paranoia and fear were ever-present in South Africa.

The fairyland-like, white, middle-class suburb where Yvette lived with her parents and sister consisted of very nice houses, well-groomed lawns, and beautifully manicured flower gardens, nurtured by the perfect climate and, of course, very cheap black labor. For me, experiencing South Africa was part-dream - because it was so beautiful and I was with Yvette - and part-nightmare, because the white minority was living on the very edge of a powder keg that could erupt into violence and revolution at any moment. Many homes were in gated communities and all homes had either barbed wire or electrified fences. Some had heavily armed white guards at the ready and everyone had barred windows on the ground floor. Some had all the above and every home had an arsenal of guns and ammunition safely locked up, so black servants could not access them.

Blacks were so completely and overwhelmingly repressed and terrorized, that most just accepted their fate and struggled to survive a day at a time. Because many had to travel long distances to work and had strenuous physical jobs (some in the diamond mines), they literally had little energy or wherewithal to revolt against their white masters. Just a few years after I departed South Africa, Nelson Mandela and others in the evolving African National Congress were sent to prison where they remained until 1992, when Apartheid finally ended.

"Sorry, master," a woman said to me, exiting an elevator she had just entered and was planning to take - until she saw me enter. She exited and had to wait until there were no 'white people' using it. Having this first person call me 'master' sent shock waves through me. I thought that addressing someone as 'master' had gone out with slavery. But this was South Africa in the early 1960s and, even though it wasn't called slavery, it appeared just as bad.

'Kaffa' is the South African synonym for 'nigger' and was used freely and indiscriminately in everyday language by whites among themselves and to intimidate blacks. As in the U.S. Deep South, white children were brainwashed from birth at home and in white schools to believe they were superior and that blacks were ignorant, dirty, diseased, and didn't deserve to be treated as equals - only as servants.

Maggie was the black woman who raised Yvette and her sister from the time they were born - when she was still a child herself. Yvette spoke so affectionately of Maggie during her year in New York that I was shocked to see the way she spoke down to her in South Africa. It was hard not to be disappointed to see the way this young woman I loved and respected treated the woman that was with her from birth.

The mantra and rationale of the whites during apartheid was: "We built this country into the richest and most modern civilization in all of Africa and we are not going to hand it over to the ignorant blacks!" And this was usually followed by: "Our blacks have the highest standard of living anywhere in Africa and they are far better off because of us."

So I thought, "Just exactly how are the blacks *better off* under this brutal white rule?"

Because of paranoia and fears of a revolution, blacks - who once lived in and around the homes of their masters - were required to travel long distances each day to and from the squalor of Soweto and other hellholes of extreme poverty festering with disease and crime, where there were few schools and hospitals, and no electricity or running water. They 'existed' in tin-roof corrugated or wood huts with no proper plumbing, the stench of raw sewage inescapable, as they sloshed barefoot through the putrid, infected, mud puddles tracking disease right into their hovels. Robbery and rape were everyday occurrences and many unemployed young black men spent their days and nights terrorizing their defenseless black neighbors. There was no law and order in the ghetto.

I could have stayed in South Africa. I came on a one-way ticket with a hundred dollars in my pocket. I would probably have married the girl, raised a family, lived a life of privilege, and I'd probably have worked for and taken over Yvette's father's business when he retired. Had the color bar not existed in such an inhumane form, I may have stayed, but the reasons to leave outweighed those to stay.

*I had a child back home, only two years old. *I should leave.*

*Here was a girl that I loved dearly and could marry; and live a life of leisure and luxury and privilege. *I should stay.*

*Apartheid went against all my values, and I would be living in a powder keg of fear and hate. My views would be considered radical and unacceptable, and if I were outspoken, I'd probably end up in prison. *I'd better leave.*

So, forty-three years later, I returned to South Africa, this time on business. Because of my deep emotional connection, I always followed South African politics and progress, and read many of the political books that were banned, like *Cry, The Beloved Country*, *George Washington September, Sir!* and *Satyagraha* by Mahatma Gandhi. I followed the life of Miriam Makeba, a famous black South African singer who lived in exile for many years for her outspoken views and her powerful songs against apartheid. Most Americans that kept up with the news knew a little about apartheid, but couldn't relate (many southerners excluded) and couldn't even pronounce the word.

Out of curiosity, when I first arrived back in Johannesburg, I opened the phone book to see if my girlfriend's father was still listed and alive, and apparently he was. I called and a young woman answered. I asked for Fritz and the girl said, "Oh, my grandfather doesn't live here any longer. I can give you his phone number if you like." She asked who I was and I told her my name. There was a moment of silence as she processed my name and said, quite excitedly, "You were my mother's American boyfriend!" Chills ran through my spine.

"Yes", I said, not realizing 'til then that I was part of their family folklore. She asked if I would like her mother's phone number, indicating that she thought her mother would be excited to hear from me. I hesitated for a moment, not having considered this possibility and said "sure", not knowing for sure if I had the nerve to call her because it could be a rejection, and that would not be pleasant.

I called her father – his granddaughter had already let him know I would be calling - and he was waiting and delighted to hear from me. He said, yes, he wanted to see me. We would get together the following week when I returned back to Jo'burg from Durban.

The big challenge was Yvette. I had serious concerns and anxiety about a possible rejection, and I had no right to expect a warm, open-armed welcome after almost half a century. I had to take a good look at myself in the mirror, which I did. I realized that, even though many years had passed, some emotional baggage had lingered on in the dark recesses of my psyche. It was a moment of truth for me as I stared at the phone and started to call many times, but each time was overtaken by fear of rejection.

I finally got up the nerve and called. Her daughter had already told her I was in town and she was delighted, saying she had been waiting to hear from me. I was so happy to hear her voice; it was like being in a dream. She sounded genuinely excited and suggested that we get together and 'catch up', if that's possible after forty years.

After a week, I returned to Johannesburg and Fritz and I spent a lovely day together, reliving our past, our mutual business interests, the people we knew, the products we sold so long ago, and how South African commerce and politics had changed over the years. We also discussed Yvette and her life, and the fact that he and his wife had thought I would have been a better choice for her. Life's irony was that they were the ones who had short-circuited her plan to return to me in the U.S.

In his late eighties, Fritz's memory was flawless; he still had a great sense of humor and loved to use off-color language, while we went through several bottles of wine. At the end of the day, after his live-in girlfriend of a similar age made us dinner, I said goodbye, knowing that I'd likely never see him again. It was a wonderful day. I will remember that day always and will always remember him as a very funny man with a great zest for life. I remember that on my first visit to Johannesburg, his two daughters and wife chided him for saying things like "I should always be able to see my girls' titties."

In contrast, he was a man who left Germany because anti-Semitism was on the rise, and Hitler and war were on the horizon; but for some unknown reason, he had a double standard and hated blacks the way Nazis hated Jews.

He was not all that thrilled with the new South Africa and the African National Congress, even though it may have represented a more secure future for his children and grandchildren. For him, the jury was still out.

Yvette came to my hotel the next day and, when she walked into the lobby, we recognized each other immediately. She looked the same, still had that creamy white complexion and peach-fuzz facial hair. Her slightly freckled face now had some wrinkles around the eyes and neck, but for the most part, she looked the same. She still had the short-cropped curly hair that I remember running my hands through while we drove down country roads in my convertible so many years before.

We had lunch at a lovely restaurant on the top of a hill, sat outside at a table that overlooked a stream - the sound of the rushing water in earshot with lush, green, rolling hills in all directions. We did our best to catch up on the forty-odd years that had passed. We spoke about our spouses, our children and about her grandson. I told her how pleased I was to see young black and white children holding hands and going to school together. Lots of positive change, but there was likely still a long way to go. Nostalgically, we recalled our weekend day trips out of Manhattan in my convertible and about her very proper, very kind, and very old German aunt and uncle in New York. We reminisced and laughed about our trip to the Berkshire Mountains and our stay at the Red Lion Inn, skinny-dipping in the pool at midnight while everyone slept.

After lunch, she drove me through downtown Johannesburg to see the changes and to see where her father's office had been for forty years. There were many beautiful new office buildings, but all had access for workers through guarded garages because the inner city was now dangerous and whites were no longer walking the streets. I'll always remember what she said over and over as we drove through town, "Look what we did to these people." I suspect her childhood bias had faded somewhat and she understood the toll that apartheid had taken on both the blacks and whites in her beloved country.

We spoke about her sister, who had moved to the U.S. many years before, and about how her parents tried to live in Boston to be near them, but couldn't bear it because they had the 'other daughter and their grandchildren' back in Johannesburg. Also, they were accustomed to the luxury of cheap black help that did not exist in Boston. They had left behind their lifetime friends, so even though they were with their younger daughter and her children in Boston, they missed their life and their other daughter in South Africa. "What fate," we thought. If her parents had allowed her to return to the U.S., she may have stayed and all the family would have been in New York or Boston, and then there would be less incentive for them to return to South Africa. "Life plays tricks," we thought and laughed like little children over our wine, sandwiches, and salad.

It was a wonderful day, perhaps one of the most memorable in my lifetime, and I do hope it was the same for her. To think that, forty-three years ago it was all cut short when I returned to the U.S., likely never to see or hear from her again. There was never any real closure for me or an official goodbye hug or kiss.

The next day, I visited her home and met her daughter and baby grandson. Her husband was a bit standoffish and likely not very happy to have me in his home, knowing that I spent a year with his wife before he met her. Anyway, I was prepared because Fritz told me all about him. Since it was a Sunday and there were cricket games on all day, I didn't see much of him, and Yvette and I were able to continue our 'catching up'.

At some point, it was time for me to go to the airport. I thought that she would take me, but she informed me at the last moment that her husband would drive me "because she had to take care of the grandchild." We hugged, kissed and said goodbye; this time I was almost certain it would be the last time I would see her as well.

It was an awkward, mostly silent ride to the airport, trying to make small talk with her husband, who was concerned with some medical problems he was having. When we pulled up to the curb, I thanked him and said goodbye, and when he drove off - leaving me standing outside the airport entrance - what came up for me was that something similar happened when I was about to leave for the airport forty-odd years earlier.

I wasn't sure why, 43 years earlier, Yvette didn't come with me to the airport and informed me at the last moment that her father would take me. "History repeating itself," I thought. I would selfishly like to believe that she couldn't face the separation then and now. Realistically, it could be that I was the only one with emotional baggage, and coming to the airport was just an inconvenience for her.

I was waiting in line to get my boarding pass and a very special calm came over me. I knew in an instant what it was. I smiled - it was something that took 43 years to attain.

The gift of closure.

THE AUSTRALIAN AND THE ROLLS

Dear Friend,

It's been some time since we last spoke and, with you being in Hong Kong, I thought I would write and share with you an extraordinary, hard-to-believe experience I had last Monday in London. As bizarre and amazing as it may seem, *it really did happen*.

I arrived in London and rang up my old friend, Arnold. Since he had also just arrived in London, he suggested that we get together for lunch. Arnold is an older wealthy gentleman still chasing the ladies, while his extremely large wife eats and drinks herself to death in their New York penthouse.

Arnold asked if I could do him a big favor: come over to his flat early on Tuesday, fetch Lisa and bring her downtown in his car, and then pick him up later for a nice lunch in Kensington Gardens. Apparently, he had some errands to run. But, looking back on that day, that was far from the case.

I first thought to ask Arnold why Lisa couldn't just hop in a cab? Then I considered that Arnold gets irritated with too many questions and he must have his reasons. So, I figured, "What the hell! Why don't I just go along with it, even though I've never driven on the wrong side of the road before?"

When I arrived in a taxi, they were both standing next

to a Rolls. I realized that this baby blue 1951 Silver Cloud convertible with the top down likely belonged to Arnold. Lisa and my eyes met and - for me, I must admit - it was a real out-of-body experience, a genuine jaw dropper!

Arnold introduced me to Lisa and, with youthful exuberance, she hopped effortlessly over the car's closed door and dropped with a bounce into the passenger seat. I thought that was rather amazing, but understandably not out of character for her.

Having driven on the right side of the road for the past fifty-five years, I was somewhat rattled and unsure of my ability to navigate the unfamiliar streets of London in this quarter-million-dollar vehicle on the wrong side of the road. It would be a serious challenge to my dexterity and concentration.

Well, I'm always up for an adventure and always looking for interesting material to launch into at cocktail parties. This is one for the books and not something someone could easily make up. But then again, they could!

Lisa is all of 90 pounds with long, streaky, platinum hair and, unfortunately, a less than congenial disposition. Because she said nothing when I greeted her, it was hard to gauge her interest in me. I was anticipating a greeting of some sort once she settled into her seat, but she looked at me with cool indifference. She squirmed about in the seat, moving her tail from this side to that.

I stepped down on the clutch, slid into first gear, waved a 'cheerio' to Arnold, and the magnificent machine effortlessly pulled away as we began our journey through the streets of London - one that I will always remember with fondness.

I navigated around the whining electric buses and ignored the impatient motorists. Pedestrians and drivers everywhere glanced at my passenger in the baby blue 1951 Silver Cloud Rolls with the top down. I did hear a few screeches and assumed it was other drivers distracted by my driving, as I continuously hit the curbs to my left and drifted into the right lane, and - of course - my fair-haired passenger likely attracted *some* attention.

Even with clear written directions, I was immediately lost - quite sure of it when I passed Harrods Department Store twice. From the Rolls, I frantically hailed a taxi. One appeared almost immediately, pulling alongside me to see what I wanted - and possibly to take a good look at my passenger. I said, "I'm lost, could I follow you to...?" and told him the address. He tipped his cap in agreement, smiled, took another look at my passenger, pulled ahead of me and I followed him down the winding, cobblestone streets for twenty minutes to our destination in the theatre district.

We arrived in front of a massive, eclectic flower shop. I tried to tip the cab driver but he refused it with a hand gesture and a smile inquiring, "May I take a photo in your Rolls with your passenger to show my friends?"

"Why, of course," I said at once, being ever so grateful for his help, as he handed me his phone and replaced me momentarily in the driver's seat for the photo op.

When he drove away, I opened the door for Lisa; she hopped out and together we entered the flower shop, an elaborate two-story glass atrium with a winding glass staircase decorated with sweet-smelling flowering vines of white, purple and red. I saw that Lisa was having a hard time going down the spiral staircase, so I helped her step by step and was greeted at the last step by the shop's proprietor.

After a few minutes, I realized that - with all the distractions - I failed to park the Rolls close enough to the curb. If a lorry or bus came by, the car would block the traffic or could be badly scratched by an impatient driver attempting to pass. I returned to the street and moved the Rolls. Just then, I noticed a young, well-dressed crowd standing outside a nearby pub consuming pizza and pints of beer. One fellow yelled out to me: "Hey, where's your wife?" and the whole group broke into hysterical, boisterous laughter, banging on the tables, making quite a racket. I had to laugh and responded, "She's chewin' the ear of the flower man," to which they broke into a second round of laughter, raised their pints and cheered me on.

The next morning, realizing that we were photographed by many on our ride through London, I found pictures of Lisa and me on the front page of a London rag. I discovered later that our images had gone viral and were now all over social media. I received a dozen emails from friends around Europe and the U.S., who recognized me as the driver, inquiring about my 'new girlfriend'.

Truth be told, Alex had thrown a big party the night before for his many London friends and business associates. He'd ordered lots of flowers and had engaged Lisa from the Australian flower man. Lisa added a very creative and 'special' touch, being an apron-wearing marsupial trained to hold a large tray of hors-d'oeuvres and remain perfectly still. She was indeed the talk of the party.

"Alex, you old devil!" I said out loud to myself. It was the best of his pranks and, as a prankster myself, I would need to go far to top this one.

Thanks, Alex!

ACKNOWLEDGEMENTS

In a chaotic world - to all my friends, acquaintances, family members, bosses, employees, teachers, and mentors who each in their own way have been 'a voice of reason'.

Thank you, one and all!